# The Art of Communication

## Romance Arts
## Book 3

### Amanda Hamm

ISBN: 978-1-943598-16-8

*The Art of Communication* is a work of fiction. All names, characters, places, events, etc. are products of the author's imagination or are used fictitiously.

More love stories by Amanda Hamm

ROMANCE ARTS
*THE ART OF INTRODUCTIONS (BOOK 1)*
*THE ART OF PATIENCE (BOOK 2)*

LOVE IN ANDAUK
*EVERYTHING OLD (BOOK 1)*
*INTO THE FIRE (BOOK 2)*
*BY ITS COVER (BOOK 3)*
*WHAT GOES AROUND (BOOK 4)*

*THEY SEE A FAMILY*
*THE STUDY GROUP* (EBOOK NOVELLA)

COFFEE AND DONUTS
*SAID AND UNSAID (BOOK 1)*
*SOFIE WAITS (BOOK 2)*
*A PERFECTLY GOOD MAN (BOOK 3)*
*NOT COMPLICATED (BOOK 4)*

STORIES FROM HARTFORD
*ANDREW'S KEY (BOOK 1)*
*JEALOUSY & YAMS (BOOK 2)*
*COLLECTING ZEBRAS (BOOK 3)*
*THE CHRISTMAS PROJECT (BOOK 4)*
*HEARTS ON THE WINDOW* (EBOOK NOVELLA)

MEET CUTE: 5 ROMANTIC SHORT STORIES

THE 4TH FLOOR LOUNGE

1

It didn't add up. Well, it did, but it didn't add up to the number on the invoice. Katie massaged an aching spot on her forehead. She'd have to ask Connie to make sense of it, not that she would.

An important part of Katie's job was making sure that each bill she paid had the costs covered by bills to corresponding customers. Those bills were sent out by coworkers in another department. If they didn't match, Katie didn't have the authority to change anything herself. It was usually fairly simple though. She could find most of the mistakes, and most of her coworkers trusted her ability to find mistakes. If she discovered that a charge had been attached to the wrong file or a couple of numbers had been transposed, she'd make the adjustment and ask someone to initial the change. Some of them did it so fast she knew they hadn't even checked her work.

Not Connie though. Sometimes it seemed as though the woman pulled numbers out of thin air. She billed multiple shipments on the same file, leaving the other files blank with no way to trace where the charges had gone. Katie had also learned long ago that the only way to get Connie's attention was to approach her in person. She sighed and pushed her chair back.

It was actually a good thing to have an excuse to stretch her legs with a walk around the office. At least it should have been, and it had been, right up until Cameron was hired to complicate the situation. No, that wasn't why he was hired. But he did complicate Katie's stroll through the building.

She had a crush on him. There was no way around admitting that. Her eyes sought him out first when she entered the room. Her pulse picked up at the prospect of any interaction. At thirty, she was mature enough to know it might be better not to act on the crush. It wasn't only by age that she had garnered that maturity. Three times in the eight years Katie had worked at EJ Industries, she'd developed romantic interest in a coworker. Twice she'd flirted her way to a date and once even worked up the courage to be the one to ask. All three times, she'd learned within a few dates that the guy was nothing like what she was looking for.

Katie preferred not to be disappointed again. She preferred to imagine that Cameron could be a great guy for her, even though imagining things didn't get her any closer to finding a husband. And it didn't get her work done. Katie sighed again, picked up her notes for Connie and headed into the hallway.

It was narrow and windowless but brightly lit. She walked under a flickering fluorescent tube. It had been flickering for at least a week. Surely someone from maintenance would have walked by and noticed it by now. Katie could put in a request herself, but it seemed too trivial out in the hallway. She'd save her complaints for when something right over her desk was flickering.

There were two closed doors before her boss's office, which was open. She looked for eye contact, preparing to smile and nod without slowing her stride to something less purposeful. He was on the phone and not paying any attention to his doorway. There were male voices coming from the next room, a shared office. Katie had a reason for not checking for eye contact there. She looked ahead to her destination. Aside from the warehouse, it was probably the largest room in the building. It had eight desks, though one of them was currently empty.

Katie turned her head immediately to her left. A guy with dark curly hair sat at the first desk on that side. His screen changed as he opened a new file. It was so fast, she wouldn't have caught it if she hadn't been looking at him as she walked in. And if she hadn't been familiar with the website that was covered, she probably wouldn't have recognized the logo in the half-second she saw it. Or did she only think she recognized the logo because she'd been staring at it a lot at home? Maybe it was something different. She gave a friendly, and she hoped completely natural, smile as she said, "Good morning, Cameron."

"Hi, Katherine." He smiled only with his eyes. But he said her name, which was sort of unusual. Most of the time, she got a plain hi or just a nod. She never heard him gabbing with anyone else so it didn't feel like a slight. He just seemed to be a very quiet guy. In the two years he'd worked there, she'd never had to question him about an invoice. Those two things were about all she knew about him. That was why she needed to stop imagining great qualities that might not exist. But he was really cute. She felt her temperature rise in the moment his eyes were on her.

Katie cooled off quickly at the irritation that flared on Connie's face when she approached her desk. She tried not to take it personally though. The woman always seemed annoyed at everyone. Katie suspected she found her job stressful because she wasn't very good at it.

"Hi, Connie," she said. "Do you have a minute?"

"I guess." Her body language said otherwise.

Katie set her notes on the desk and pointed at some numbers as she spoke. "I can't find where you billed these two charges from Central. I thought you might have included them on this file, but it's still too high so either I'm wrong or you included something else, too. Can you break down for me what's billed on this file, and write down where these two ended up?"

Connie pulled the note closer and began to scribble on it. She appeared to be writing down a version of what Katie had just said. For later. She wasn't going to look up anything right then, not that Katie would have wanted to stand there while she did. Her eyes scanned over Connie's desk. There were two pictures of two different kids. She assumed they were both Connie's, though she thought it was strange she didn't just have one family portrait. Strange but not wrong. Both the kids looked like young teens, but the same pictures had been there for years so there was no telling how old they were in real life.

Connie looked up as she finished writing. Her expression asked if there was anything else and threatened to feel greatly burdened if there was.

"While I'm here," Katie started anyway, "I wondered if you've had a chance to look at the numbers I gave you the other day?"

There was a huge eye roll as Connie began to dig through her messy in-box. She pulled out a sticky note with handwriting Katie recognized as her own. "This it?" she asked. She didn't take her eyes off the paper so Katie didn't bother nodding. Connie frowned at what she read, sighed heavily, set it down and wrote "today" with three underlines before she stuck it back in the tray.

At least the request was on top now. That was about as much as Katie expected. "Thanks," she said. "I'll get back to my office now." She smiled patiently and offered a quick wave.

Katie got nods and greetings from a few other people as she left the office, including a commiserating smile from an older man. There was no more interaction from Cameron though. He was focused on his work. She liked to think that showed dedication and strong ethics and not zero interest in the old woman walking by. It might not have been maturity alone that kept Katie from trying to talk to him more. It might have had something to do with her suspicion that he would reject her.

****

4

Katie was at home enjoying her Saturday off. She was trying to enjoy the day off anyway. She was super fidgety. She was sitting on a loveseat with the footrest out and a book in her lap. Her finger was marking the page she'd given up on reading for the moment. A laptop was lying on the seat next to her, calling to her.

Katie picked up her bookmark and stuck it in the page to free her hands. She reached for the laptop but stopped herself before she actually touched it. Did she really want to do this? She pulled back her hand, laced her fingers together and closed her eyes. Did God want her to do this? Was the decision leaving her unsettled or simply nervous?

Just because it was the day after she thought she might have seen the logo on Cameron's screen didn't make it a rash decision. She'd been thinking about it for months, pretty much since she saw her thirtieth birthday on her calendar. She didn't want to be single forever. It was a good idea to try to do something to change being single. Yes, it was a good idea.

She moved the laptop closer without opening it. Her fingers brushed along the edge, following the seam, while she continued to talk herself into the next step. When she lifted the top, the Courting Catholics homepage appeared. The blue and white logo at the top was a sketched representation of Mary and Joseph. Katie moved the little arrow to the join button and let it hover.

Buzzing from across the room told her she was getting a call from a family member. She closed the laptop with relief at another delay. Her sister Cecelia was behind the call.

"Hey, Cecelia, how are you feeling?" Cecelia was six-months pregnant. Asking a pregnant woman how she was feeling was usually a good way to begin a conversation. It was kind of like saying, "I know being pregnant is constantly on your mind, and I'm happy to let you talk about it."

"Pretty good," Cecelia said. "I wore maternity clothes all week, and it finally felt right."

Katie smiled at the statement. Cecelia had been complaining for about two months that all her clothes were her enemies. She said that regular clothes made her look fat or were uncomfortable because she was fat, and that maternity clothes made her look as though she was trying to cover up fat by pretending to be pregnant. Katie was happy to hear that her sister might be moving past a self-conscious stage. "Good," she said. "I know that blue top already looks great on you and has some room for more tummy."

"Which blue one?"

"Uh… white flowers, button front."

"Oh, right. Yeah, I like that one," Cecelia said. "I borrowed it from Liz."

Liz was the sister in between Katie and Cecelia. She was twenty-seven and had a boy and a girl and a husband who would do anything for all of them. Cecelia was twenty-three, had been married for barely a year, and was already a few months from motherhood. They also had a 28-year-old brother whose toddler was the spitting image of his wife. It was impossible to tell who was who in side-by-side pictures. It was crazy, about as crazy as how jealous all of Katie's siblings made her with their budding families. Even her youngest brother, who was as single as she was. He was twenty and still in school. She was jealous of how many years he had before anyone said he was *still* single.

"Speaking of Liz," Cecelia continued, "she's why I called. She told me you had Mom's box of ornaments."

"What ornaments?" Katie was teasing. She knew what ornaments.

"The supplies for the little angels with the cross-stitched dresses we each have. Obviously. I think you knew what I meant. I thought Mom said she was going to have each of us make them for our own kids and give them to her so I thought Liz would have them since she has the youngest grandchild, right now, but she said you made all three of the new ones."

The teasing mood left as Katie felt the sting of accusation in those words. "Uh, yeah, I did."

"How did that happen?" Cecelia asked.

"I don't know. I mean, Liz just asked me."

"Why are you the designated angel maker?"

"I'm not." Katie felt oddly defensive for having done a few favors. Was there about to be some family drama over Christmas ornaments?

"Have you already started one for *my* baby?"

"No," Katie said, hoping that the one-word answer was the right one.

"Good. I want to do it," Cecelia said. "Why did you make Liz and Michael's?"

"Because they asked me to."

"Really?" Her tone was highly skeptical.

Katie couldn't tell if she didn't believe they'd asked her or didn't understand why. She resigned herself to giving all the details. "Well, you know Calli was born in December and Liz had a slow recovery. She realized like a week before Christmas that she hadn't made an ornament and asked if I would do it for her. Then I think Michael asked Mom if she would make his and since I already had the supplies the request transferred to me. Liz buttered me up with compliments about how I'd done such a nice job on Calli's and… Do you want the box?"

"Hmm." Cecelia made an angry noise that sounded like grudging acceptance of facts she hadn't approved. She'd always been the most emotional one in the family.

Katie tried to figure out how to politely tell her sister she was making a big deal out of nothing. "Why are we even talking about Christmas ornaments in the summer? You know it's barely July, right?"

"Well, I…" She let out a short laugh, heading off her own tantrum before it started. She might have a quick temper, but she wasn't completely unreasonable. "I saw an ad for some Christmas in July sale happening next week, and it got me thinking about how this will be my first Christmas as a mom and how the little one will be too little to remember it or even really do anything special and I thought about how we'd at least have a special ornament to... I thought if I worked on it now, I could present it to Mom as a way of announcing the name and everything."

"That would be nice," Katie said.

"So can you bring me the box sometime?"

"Sure. I'll dig it out of the closet and put it where I'll remember it next time I see you."

"Great. Okay. See ya." Cecelia hung up.

Katie set her phone down and looked at the laptop where she'd left it on the loveseat. She stepped closer and continued to stare it down. She was going to join and set up her profile today. The decision had been made, and it was a good one. Katie wanted to get married, and she felt certain God wanted that for her, too. Looking at guys who wanted to be husbands could only help. She glanced at her bedroom. That box of ornaments Cecelia wanted was on a shelf in the closet. She really didn't have to dig it out of anywhere. It would take only a few seconds to get it down. She'd just do that first.

2

Katie sat at her kitchen table with her laptop open. One more click and she'd be a member of Courting Catholics. Signing up was the easy part. Even with Katie's frugal nature, the fee was nothing. It was creating a profile that she dreaded. But she'd made it this far. Eventually.

It was amazing how many quick little things Katie had found to fill up her Saturday and put off this task one more day. Now she'd been to church and had a formerly frozen enchilada on a plate next to her. She was giving herself a tiny bite as a reward for each blank she completed. She clicked submit and tasted a bite of spicy chicken, only a small bite. She couldn't finish her lunch before she finished her project.

On the other side of her laptop was a notepad where for months she'd been jotting down information about herself, then scribbling it out, then rewording it. Some of the blanks were easy. First name. Age. Katie didn't mind sharing the basics. Anything else was difficult to put into words. That enchilada wasn't enticing enough to bare even a glimpse of her soul. She was dying of curiosity though. She wanted to skip to the part where she started reading the guys' profiles. That would not only be unfair, but also unrealistic. No one was going to show interest in a nearly blank profile, and she wouldn't blame them.

Katie looked at her food. It was getting cold. And she wasn't getting any younger. She'd already spent two months thinking about what she would write. She only had to do it. With the fee paid, the clock was ticking. Katie stopped making excuses and began typing words that had been playing in the back of her mind, the things she thought a potential match should know. The picture was the real stumbling block. It was the primary reason she'd been putting this off.

Selfies were not Katie's thing. She had no pictures of herself before about three weeks ago, when she'd realized she'd need a decent picture for this site. Now she had a good collection. But it was good only if she considered the number of pictures and not the quality. She had repeatedly flipped through her attempts with unfounded optimism that what had looked awful when she took it would suddenly work for her. Then she'd added more bad pictures.

Katie started at the beginning. Her hair looked nice in most of the pictures. Liz had recently talked Katie into some golden highlights in her otherwise plain brown hair. It was subtle, but she liked it. Unfortunately, it was about the only thing she liked about any of the pictures. Katie knew she couldn't smile naturally on cue so she'd tried to appear pleasant without smiling. She looked bored, bored out of her mind. So she'd tried smiling. There was a crazed expression on top of each forced smile. One even resembled the snarl of a rabid dog.

Then she came to the fake candid shots. She had tried to take pictures of herself reading a book or doing a puzzle since she had listed those activities under hobbies. How had she thought that would appear unposed? It was clear she was the one holding the camera and deliberately turned away from it. Plus, a profile was more like a mug shot than anything flattering.

The pictures got even worse. In what had been a moment of desperate lunacy, Katie had tried to use her glasses as a prop. She had the same tortoise shell frames for about six years and generally liked them, at least as much as anyone liked a pair of glasses. She had no idea what made her take them off and hold them in front of her face. Was it supposed to look like she was trying to clean them? Why would anyone take a picture of that? The next shot had the glasses perched on top of her head, which was something she never did. It was completely inane. She couldn't see very well with glasses nowhere near her eyes and moving them did nothing to improve the lost expression. Was that an attempt to appear thoughtful? She looked as though she didn't know what the buttons did and took a picture by accident. And they looked like reading glasses on top of her head. She didn't need to do anything to make herself look older. But even that was better than the one with the earpiece between her teeth.

A morbid thought shook Katie's brain. What if she died in some freak accident tomorrow and her siblings went through these pictures for her obituary? No matter how unlikely, the idea was frightening enough to cause her to delete all but a handful of the least awkward pics. She might have to start over on getting something for her profile, but she was too impatient to do it right away. Or scared. She added a note stating that she was new and still deciding which picture to add, then submitted the profile without one to move on to the part that she hoped would be more fun.

A couple of suggested profiles popped up. One of the guys was definitely not bad looking. Katie tried not to read too many details about him. She planned to do this methodically and not based on appearance. Noting that the guy with the nice smile lived in Texas did help her turn away from him faster.

Katie started a search to include only guys whose devotion to the faith was as strong as hers. She didn't like the term deal-breaker, but anything less would be a source of constant friction and stress in a relationship. Geography was the next limiter. While Katie thought she might be willing to relocate, she wanted to start with guys who wouldn't make her cross that bridge. She lived in the very small town of Andauk, OH. The place she worked was about halfway between Andauk and another small town called Tindee. Including both would improve her chances of finding someone. The fact that Cameron was more likely to live in Tindee, since she'd never see him outside work, also motivated her to include that town.

Only three results showed up. The first guy was fifty-three. That was only a year younger than Katie's dad. The second guy was less appealing. His hands were up in the air and his tongue wagged out the side of his mouth in a picture that seemed like someone trying way too hard to look like a lot of fun, and not Katie's idea of fun. What she could see of his profile had no capitalization and words that were horribly misspelled or not real words. Other red flags indicated that the profile was either some sort of scam or created by a complete idiot. Katie would have dismissed him quickly even if she wasn't chomping at the bit to investigate the first thing she'd noticed when the results appeared. The third guy's name was Cameron.

She brought up the full profile and tried to take it all in at once. There was no last name to confirm this was the Cameron West she knew from work. She'd expected that, but there was no picture either. This could easily be a different guy named Cameron. He was twenty-four. That lined up with what she might know about the other Cameron. She remembered someone who may or may not have been well-informed saying he'd been hired straight out of college. If he'd been twenty-two when he graduated, which would have been two years ago, it would all add up. But there was a lot of speculation in that math.

Katie read through all the other information. Several times. He described his social life as a weekly game of Tichu with three close friends. He said it was predictable and consistent fun. She appreciated what some people might consider an oxymoron. It was clear by his wording that he was aware of that perception. Though Katie had never heard of Tichu, she did enjoy games. She used to play more with her family before the grandkids became the center of every get together.

The guy shared an apartment. He wrote, "My roommate works nights and seems to intentionally sleep when I'm home. There are usually a few minutes when he returns from work and I'm about to leave when we can talk if necessary and otherwise ignore each other. It's a perfect situation to lower my rent while I save up to invest in a life I can actually share with someone. I hope to never have to leave myself a reminder to ask my wife the next time I see her if it's my turn to buy mustard."

It was funny yet serious. Katie almost laughed out loud. It probably wasn't that funny, but she just really liked everything she read about this guy. The problem was that she was picturing these words typed by the Cameron she knew. It felt dangerous to connect the two in her mind when the connection might only exist in her mind. Why didn't he have a picture!?

Yes, it was wrong to find that frustrating when she was just as guilty. And it was even more frustrating that it could be a good thing. As much as she wanted to know what he looked like, she couldn't help but think he might not have a picture because he could relate to her struggle to find a good one.

Katie was both thrilled and terrified by the profile. What if it was the Cameron she knew? And what if it wasn't? If it was, he'd end up rejecting her. He'd shown no interest at all in person. And if it was someone else, would she be disappointed when she didn't have the same physical reaction when she saw him? That shouldn't matter. What was important was that their personalities were compatible. This online Cameron had scored the same as Katie on the personality quiz.

She continued to reread his information over and over as though something might change and tell her what to do. Eventually, she decided that the first step would be to reheat that enchilada she'd forgotten about. The second step, apparently, was to fantasize about meeting this guy, finding out he was Cameron West, and having him admit he'd been secretly noticing her all along. A hot bite brought her back to reality with a burned tongue.

It would have been easier if she'd found a profile that was definitely Cameron with information that ruled him out and cured her obsession. Then she could have searched this site as she'd intended before she got a hint he might be on it. Maybe that was still a possibility. It occurred to Katie that her narrow search might have eliminated his profile. She marked the unknown Cameron for later consideration and opened up the faith questions in her search and included a wider geographic range. Her eyes were tired by the time she skimmed through the new results. There were two other Camerons, both with pictures to show they were strangers.

Katie closed the laptop and stepped away from it to clear her head. It didn't work. Her head remained crammed full of possible ways this could play out. Maybe she should add a picture of herself before she messaged him so he could "anonymously" tell her they were a poor match. No. It would be impossible to go to work not knowing if Cameron knew something he thought she didn't. The uncertainty would drive her insane. Or just cause her to act neurotic around him, which might be just as bad.

She returned to her computer and searched social security records. How popular was the name Cameron twenty-four years ago? What were the odds this was the same guy? Was there a way to determine the percentage of Catholic families in the area? Were these lists sorted by state? Katie had made several statistical notes before she slammed the lid closed and laughed at her deep dive down the rabbit hole. There were too many variables to make math helpful in this situation. Even high or low odds would leave doubts.

Should she just ignore that profile? Katie propped her elbows on the table and let her face fall onto her hands. He was clearly her best starting point on the matches, better than the old guy or the idiot. She closed her eyes and prayed. *God, give me the strength to do this*. And there was her answer. As soon as she realized she was asking for courage rather than direction, she knew where God was leading. It wasn't complicated until it was complicated. This guy might never message her back. And they might mutually decide not to meet in person. Maybe the truth of whether or not they knew each other would come out naturally. Katie would wrestle with options when they needed wrestling. For now, she typed out a simple message.

*Hi. Your profile was the first one to catch my eye. I don't like mustard so it would always be your turn. Are you interested in talking?*

It was a ridiculous mess. Katie drove to work Monday morning having not responded to anyone in her family and still not wanting to respond. Her mom had sent several texts letting Katie know that she appreciated how she'd stepped up to make the Christmas ornaments for her siblings and that she felt remiss in not saying so sooner. One of them had suggested that it would be nice if the same person made all of the grandkids' ornaments for consistency and simplicity and to make sure the supplies never got lost in the shuffle. She hinted that Katie could volunteer to take on that responsibility. Cecelia had texted Katie to thank her sarcastically for making her feel guilty about wanting to do something for her own child. Then Michael asked Katie if it was her fault that people were yelling at him about Christmas ornaments in July. Liz sent a message to everyone stating for the record that if she had any more kids, she didn't care who made the ornaments as long as it wasn't Noah.

She was kidding of course. But Noah, the youngest, had been completely out of the loop and replied to her group text with a question mark. That opened the whole thing up to a total rehash. Katie stuck the phone and the two unread texts in her desk drawer as soon as she got to work so she wouldn't have to think about it. It made her roll her eyes. She wondered if she should plan on handing off the box to Cecelia when no one else was looking.

There was a sticky note on her desk about a call to return and a stack of mail that had arrived on Saturday. Part of Katie's job was to open the paper bills and distribute them to the others who shared her office. She wasn't sure exactly when that became part of her job. Everyone had taken turns when she first started. Katie had gradually gotten more turns until no one else had one. She didn't mind though. It was better than waiting for someone else to do it, and she was generally happy being productive.

It was, overall, not a bad Monday. Or Tuesday. She actually made it until Wednesday before she had to bother people about their record-keeping. Of course, there were four people to bother and one of them was Connie. Katie managed to enter that room feeling no more uncomfortable than normal. She didn't think anyone noticed how many times her eyes went to Cameron, and her mind only briefly went to the online version and whether or not he could be the same guy.

It probably helped that she'd gotten no reply. She had received two messages from other guys on the site. They were both easy to reject based on the information they provided. Well, they were easy to reject mentally. She still felt bad telling them she wasn't interested.

By Saturday, she had mostly given up on online Cameron and determined to take some action. She was calling this phase two in her head. Surely if she broadened her search to include Toledo and Sandusky, she would find promising matches that were still not too far away. She planned to see what style of photos they had – candid activities or straight headshots or something else – and use a similar picture of herself, no matter how bad it turned out. Maybe some guy would be pleasantly surprised to find out that she was simply allergic to cameras and capable of smiling in person.

But when Katie sat down to implement phase two, she found a message from Cameron.

**Hello. Sorry it took me so long to reply. I was surprised to get your message because I thought removing the picture**

*would discourage interest. (Because I would seem shady, not because the picture was that great.) I planned to take a break after some bad experiences. Curiosity is getting the better of me though, especially since you are the closest geographically that I have 'met.' Do you want to tell me a bit more about yourself?*

Katie closed her laptop. She calmly walked the length of her apartment and back. Then she jumped up and down very fast about a dozen times. With the nervous energy out of the way, she returned to her chair to consider what to write. She didn't think work Cameron knew much more about her than she knew about him. She could be fairly open without worrying about revealing that he knew her as Katherine from accounting, if in fact he did. Starting a conversation with this online Cameron would probably get him to mention where he worked before he suggested meeting. Probably. That was Katie's hope anyway. She would write to him as though he was already a friend, and perhaps he would become one. What happened next, or didn't happen, was in God's hands.

*Cameron,*
*I guess I will start by telling you about my family. They are important to me even though they are driving me nuts at the moment. I am the oldest of five. Our parents raised us in the Church, and we are all still active. I was even the Confirmation sponsor for two of my siblings. My mom made a Christmas angel for each of us after we were born. They're ornaments she hangs on her tree. The angels have cloth faces with thread for hair over craft stick arms and legs and a dress made out of cross-stitch fabric. Mom stitched sprigs of holly on the front of the dresses around our names and dates of birth. These are cherished keepsakes for her.*

*Now you might have some questions. Why am I giving you all these details about Christmas ornaments? Why am I even thinking about Christmas in the middle of the summer? Well, I think the best way to illustrate my family might be to tell you why they're all getting on my nerves. I want you to be able to picture what they're all talking about. Stick with me while I delve into a little more backstory.*

*At some point, maybe even right after she made the first one, my mom decided that she wanted one to represent each of her eventual grandchildren as well. It was decided that each of us should make the ornaments for our own kids, then give them to Mom. How was this decided? It depends who you ask. I remember my mom telling me that she was afraid by the time her youngest kid had his youngest kid, her fingers might no longer cooperate with some of the smaller work. Or maybe it would be hard on her eyes. She thought it would be better to pass it off early rather than having to give up only on the last baby or two.*

*But my sister Cecelia claims that our mom told her she wanted us to make them because after she dies, we can each take the one she made for us and the ones we made for our kids and they can someday make more and continue the tradition.*

*My brother Noah insists that our other sister Liz wanted to make an angel for her baby, the first grandkid, because she was due only two weeks before Christmas and wanted to make sure the ornament was ready on time without having to tell Mom the name before the baby was born. Liz did make a big deal out of keeping the name a secret – she must have told us a dozen times in the last month of the pregnancy that they had a name they weren't telling anyone – but she doesn't remember asking for the ornament supplies or particularly wanting to make it herself.*

*At any rate, Liz had the box that December three years ago because it had somehow been decided that she should make her own baby's angel ornament. Okay, are you still interested? Were you ever? We're almost caught up to where I get dragged in, though I didn't know it was going to be an issue at the time. I was visiting with Liz a few days after the baby was born. She was not feeling very well. I was there to* help her tidy up a bit and asked if there was anything else I could do for her. She admitted she hadn't started on that angel before the baby came and knew she'd never get it done before Christmas. She asked if I thought I had time for it. I took the box home with me.

(Let me break here to pretend this is some sort of legal document. From here on, whenever I mention "the box," I mean the box that contains supplies for making my mom's special angel ornaments.)

I spent several hours making an angel for Liz. She thanked me. Mom got it in time to hang on the tree that Christmas Eve. We always do the tree Christmas Eve. And I thought everyone knew I had made it or didn't care who made it.

Fast forward one year. My brother Michael and his wife had a baby that October. Should I pause to give you the order? When I talk about my siblings, people always seem to want to know who's older than whom. It's me, then Michael, then Liz, then Cecelia, and Noah last. About a week before Christmas, I got a call from Michael. Mom had called him to make sure he was getting the ornament ready for his little one. Apparently, he had no idea that anyone had decided anything about Mom not making all of them. She told him that I had the box. Rather than ask for the box, Michael asked if I would just make it for him.

I didn't mind. I would have preferred to have more than a few days, but they're kind of fun to make so it was fine. His wife pulled me aside Christmas Day to thank me. She confessed it had been her idea for Michael to ask me because he wanted her to do it, and she was afraid she'd mess up an important tradition. I consider her a friend, but that was probably the first real sisterly moment we've had in the five years they've been married. It was nice.

Last year, Liz had her second baby. He came in early November so she did not wait until the last minute to ask me about an angel for him. She remembered I had the box, and asked me about it one of the first times I got to hold the new arrival. She showered me with ridiculous flattery about how my ability to thread a needle was unmatched and if anyone could stitch the right date, it would be me. She made me laugh so I was happy to help her again.

Now it's Cecelia's turn. She's expecting her first in October, and she's already thinking about her baby's angel. That's why the rest of us have to think about it. She didn't know I had the box. She didn't know that Liz and Michael hadn't made the ornaments for their kids. I'm not sure how she missed that, but I didn't think it was going to be a problem. She calmed down as soon as I told her I had no intention of making her ornaments for her if she didn't want me to.

Then the texts were flying. My mom was concerned that the box was going to get lost if we started shuttling it between households to make the ornaments. Cecelia was mad at everyone for changing the tradition without consulting her. Mom suggested making ornaments was a good role for me. She didn't mean to offend me, but it sounded as though she was saying I was the old spinster aunt who would never have any kids of my own. It's on my profile, but in the interest of honest communication, I should point out that I still hope the family God intends for me includes a few kids. Meanwhile, Michael kept sending group texts asking everyone to please leave him out of the group texts.

Things settled down after a couple days. Cecelia admitted that as long as she could make her own ornaments, it shouldn't bother her if her siblings didn't want to. I brought the box to my parents' house last night. We all gather there for dinner about once a month. I pointed out to Cecelia that I was leaving it by the door for her to take home.

We had a nice dinner. My dad usually does the cooking. I think my own cooking is fine, though I never try to make anything too involved or elaborate. Michael announced that he and his wife are expecting a second child in January. Naturally, we're all very happy for them. But I have to be honest, I was most happy that no one said anything about who was going to make that child's Christmas ornament. I'll do it if anyone asks, but I'm not going to be the one to bring it up. I'm out.

Except that I'm not out. The box has disappeared. I found three texts from Cecelia this morning, two she sent late last night, asking where exactly I put the box. As though she didn't watch me put it down. My mom also asked me to check my car, just in case I left it there and only imagined that I brought it in with me. It took me a few conversations to piece together why people were bugging me.

I left before Cecelia last night. I didn't look to see if the box was still where I put it because I thought I was done thinking about it for at least a few months. The box was not there when Cecelia left. No one seems to know what happened. The blame has, for now, shifted from me to my dad. The working theory is that he must have put it away somewhere without realizing what it was. He has no memory of moving the box, but that hasn't stopped my mom from tearing the house apart trying to figure out where he put it.

Cecelia's mad at everyone again. She's upset that some of us are not taking it seriously. Although Michael did joke that someone broke into the house just to steal a box of craft supplies because it's so valuable, and he should have known Cecelia wouldn't be amused. I admit I would be disappointed if the box is really lost. I'm just not as prone to getting worked up. I'm sure it's going to turn up somewhere.

But I'm going to have to leave you with this huge cliffhanger right now. Let me know if you have any interest in knowing how it turns out. I would also enjoy hearing about the game in your profile, Tichu. I don't know anything about it, and I've refrained from searching it up so I can get a fully biased opinion from someone who plays regularly. If you want to tell me about those bad experiences you mentioned, that might be good, too. I could kind of self-select out if I know I'd be

*guilty of something similar. Here's hoping for a positive response.*
  *Katie*

Katie spent the next few hours trying not to analyze what she'd written. Was it wise to start by focusing on her being the oldest when he might already be thinking thirty was the edge of his acceptable range? Did her tone come off as disrespectful to her family members rather than light and teasing? Was her long letter boring? Was he rolling his eyes at her for sharing the family drama? The more she tried not to think any of those questions, the more often they came into her head.

She had finished and sent off her message just before lunch. She refused to check for a reply until near the end of the day. It seemed a good idea to wait and be disappointed once instead of several times throughout the day. When she was thinking about getting ready for bed, Katie reminded herself that she should wait at least a few days before she gave up, then opened her computer.

There was a message from Cameron. She gasped and jumped up before she read any of it. Just because he replied didn't mean it was good. He may have said he'd heard enough to know they wouldn't get along. He might try to make it impersonal, that he'd reconsidered and needed a longer break. It could be a good response though. And that was just as scary because she was still picturing Cameron from work behind it. If it was him, this was not going to end well. Katie was excited about the idea that it could be him, and that was exactly why it wasn't going to end well.

She rubbed her hands together and blew out a calming breath. She tried to look at the message without reading any of it. It was long! That had to be good. This won't work was only three words. He enjoyed her message! He mentioned "the box." There were names she didn't recognize. Katie closed her eyes for a moment, tried to relax, and started at the beginning.

Katie,

Thank you for the long message. I really enjoyed hearing about your family. I am an only child. Your talk of siblings somehow made me glad I don't have any and jealous at the same time. It was great how you snuck in details about yourself surrounded by a funny story. Much more informative and intriguing than a list of facts would have been. I am curious to know what happened to "the box" and hope we can stay in touch long enough for me to find out.

As for your questions, I will do my best. The first bad experience I had here won't be repeated unless you are lying. I exchanged several messages with a woman who listed her age on her profile as thirty-five. I was already wondering if that age difference would be a problem. It'd be enough to maybe have different perspectives on some things, and we'd have to address the elephant of fertility sooner than later. I feel totally awkward even hinting at that sort of thing in print. But she seemed nice, and I'd been messaging women for nearly six months with no luck. When we met in person, it was immediately obvious that she'd used an old picture. We couldn't talk about anything because all I could think was "How old are you really?" Eventually, I got frustrated and blurted out the question. She got defensive and danced around the subject before saying she was forty-one. I didn't believe her, and the fact that I couldn't was worse than the age. It made me doubt everything she'd said in her messages. Honesty is very important to me.

The second bad experience happened pretty soon after that. I was messaged by someone about a hundred miles away. I didn't think we'd be meeting anytime soon, but a few messages wouldn't hurt. She said her membership was about to expire and asked for my number. There weren't any red flags on her profile. We had a brief friendly conversation after we exchanged numbers. I had to work the next day, and I keep my phone off at work. I do usually check it during lunch, and I'm not sure why I didn't that day. When I turned it on as soon as I got home, I found fifty-three texts from her. About half were random comments about her day and the

*other half were questions about why I was ignoring her. I
tried to suggest we agree on a time of day I'd be available to
chat. That offended her and resulted in a barrage of texts
asking why I had joined a dating site if I didn't want to pursue
a real relationship and that I had misrepresented my
intentions and... I blocked her.*

*On to more pleasant topics. Tichu. That's one of my favorite
topics. I am so impressed that you have the self-control not to
look it up. You might have gotten incorrect information from
people who don't like it. Allow me to share the truth. The
game is complicated but not difficult. Have you heard that
quote about the Bible? The one that says it's shallow enough
for a mouse to wade and deep enough for an elephant to
swim? (I should find the source.) Tichu is similar in that you
could follow all the rules and still lose every time. There is
strategy, but the right play might depend on what other
players are holding, and of course you don't know what
they're holding so there's an unpredictability that keeps it
challenging.*

*I play every Friday night with the same three guys. Trevor is
the one who invited me. We went to school together, were
both in a gaming group through campus ministry. We kind of
bonded over how many people came in and were like, "Oh,
you play board games," then left. We agreed they were
missing out. We bumped into each other again about a year
after graduation. I mentioned that I missed the regular
games, and he said he wanted a weekly Tichu game but
needed a fourth guy. The timing was awesome for both of us.
Trevor probably takes the game most seriously of all of us,
almost appears to be in pain when he realizes he might have
misplayed something.*

*One of the other guys is someone I knew from campus
ministry, too. His name is Logan. Nice guy, but super
fidgety. He can't stop himself from grabbing the cards at the
end of the round no matter whose turn it is to shuffle. Did I
mention that Tichu is a card game? I won't tell you what the
cards look like unless you ask.*

*The last guy is Ryan. He's Trevor's brother. I was surprised when I met him because I recognized him from the choir at my church. To be clear, I mean only that I'd seen him in the choir. I do not sing in the choir. I do not sing period. God did not bless me with that talent. I mentioned to Ryan how I knew him. He said he was an unapologetic choir boy. I guess it's a pet peeve of his when people use that as an insult. We chatted briefly that it's a shame integrity has become a bad word in some circles. Heavy stuff for an introduction, which makes me wonder if I shouldn't be mentioning it here. It's not as entertaining as your message. But it's the first thing that came into my head when I tried to describe Ryan.*

*I like how you ended your message with questions because it gave me something to write about. Would you think I'm horribly shallow if I ask what you look like? Now that we've begun to connect without pictures, I'm pretty nervous about putting mine back. I will if you will. If you'd rather just describe yourself, that'd be okay for now.*

*What kind of books do you read? How do you feel about your job? Is it something you do to afford a life or is it your life? Do you do anything active? You listed your financial style as mostly frugal. What would you consider a worthy splurge? Would you rather ignore my questions and tell me what you think I should know?*
    *Cameron*

4

She drummed her fingers on the table. Three days should be enough. It might be too much, but there wasn't anything she could do about it if it was. Was there a perfect time to come off as an eager correspondent rather than a desperate nutjob? Or was it all about the content of the messages?

Katie had been tempted to write out a response to Cameron's letter the moment she finished reading it. She knew she wouldn't be quick though. She'd end up staying awake later than normal and risk crankiness at work, both of which were not like her. It was important to be true to herself while starting a new relationship. Not that a few messages was a relationship.

An immediate response might have been a bad impression, too. He'd said he was turned off by the woman who sent him a bazillion messages. This would have been different but still had the potential to be overwhelming. Especially if she included all the thoughts running through her head. There was so much to process. He'd been hesitant but not opposed to meeting someone thirty-five so thirty was probably not that scary to him. Probably. There had been some serious points included, but the bit about incorrect opinions on Tichu made her literally laugh out loud. It sounded as though he sincerely enjoyed her story. Katie had growing hopes that this guy was someone she could get along with very well.

Her concerns about what he looked like were also growing though. She could not stop herself from picturing the Cameron from work when she thought of his message. A message that said honesty was important to him. She'd given it some thought and prayer and decided that not saying she *suspected* they *might* know each other in person was not the same as hiding something she actually knew.

If it was the same Cameron, it would be embarrassing to admit she'd caught a glimpse of his screen because she was trying to see him before she even got into the room. And if it was a different Cameron, he'd probably prefer not to hear about her crushing on a coworker. Katie needed proof one way or the other first.

A physical description seemed like a possible route to the truth. He'd asked for one of her. Katie believed her appearance was bland enough that she could give plenty of detail without giving away who she was in real life, *if* she was someone he'd recognize. Doing so would prompt him to reciprocate, and then she would know if his appearance matched what she was imagining. She'd spent the last two days – not the whole days but significant portions – drafting and editing another long message. It was time to send it.

*Cameron,*
*You've given me some great material. I'm going to start with the question with the most potential for disappointment and see if I can work my way up to something that's actually interesting. I'm not comfortable sharing a picture right now. I hope you can understand that after confessing a similar feeling. As for description, I think I'm five foot four, pretty thin. If your question about whether or not I do anything active was intended to find out if I'm an athletic type, the answer is no. I have an exercise bike that I ride regularly to keep from being a complete couch potato. But I do not have the coordination or skills to be competent at anything beyond riding a bike. For what it's worth, I can honestly say I don't remember the last time I fell off one. I would also have to admit I don't know how long it's been since I rode one capable of tipping over so it might not be worth much.*

*I have brown hair. It's mostly straight and just long enough that it sometimes stays behind my shoulders. My eyes are brown, and I wear glasses. My skin is pretty pale. Both my parents have mostly Irish heritage, though there are no redheads in the immediate family. I don't think I have any distinctive features, and I usually dress fairly plain. I don't spend much on clothes, which I mention only as a segue. You asked what I would consider a good splurge. I guess I'd say I lean towards spending on experiences more than stuff. I'd sooner buy a concert ticket than an upgrade of something I already have. A family vacation would probably be my biggest splurge, but even then I'd look for fun activities closer to home to save on travel expenses.*

*I don't hate my job. If you're asking if I'm a workaholic, no. I have regular hours and leave work at work. My ideal would be to take at least a few years off if I ever have kids. I've been trying to build a nest egg to allow for that.*

*Tichu sounds... intimidating. You say there are right moves that change based on the circumstances? How long did it take you to learn the game? Do the cards have numbers or pictures? Do you play them in front of you or on each other's cards? Do you have a full hand or only one card at a time? I still haven't searched it so you can interpret any of those questions as me asking what the cards look like. I would love to give it a try someday.*

*What kind of books do I read? Mostly faith-based nonfiction. There is always something new to learn. I do mix in some fluff, too. I like a good historical Christian romance, particularly with a side of humor. I haven't recently, but every now and then I'll grab a free ebook from some unknown author. It's a gamble, like watching B movies. Sometimes I'll find a hidden gem, sometimes it'll be so bad it's good. And sometimes, it's just the kind of bad where your brain will be mad at you if you read too long. I think I've been off that kick because I got too many of the last category in a row.*

Do you want me to tell another funny family story? I guess if you don't, you can stop reading. This happened back when I was in college. I came home most weekends. One weekend, I came home to find that Liz and Cecelia were arguing over the fairies. Liz used to have a fairy collection. (I think she still has it, just tucked away somewhere.) It wasn't a specific set or brand. It was maybe between twenty and thirty little statues of various materials, and she kept them all spread out on the desk in her room.

As an aside, it used to bug my mom that she'd gotten each of us a desk for homework, and I was the only one who used it for homework. Michael always had a stack of clothes he hadn't gotten around to putting away. The others just had clutter of some kind in the way. But as long as the homework was getting done somewhere, she didn't really give anyone a hard time.

Anyway, Liz had accused Cecelia of playing with her fairies without asking because some of them had been moved. Cecelia insisted she hadn't touched them. They shared a room, and it wasn't uncommon for something like that to come up so I didn't really pay much attention. Until they were still arguing about it the next weekend. I couldn't believe it had gone on so long. When I asked my mom about it, she said they weren't still arguing, they were arguing again. Apparently, they'd both let it go most of the week, but Liz had just noticed that the fairies had been moved again.

This was when it seemed a little weird. Cecelia has always been the type to wear her emotions on her sleeve. That made it easy to spot when she was lying. She seemed completely sincere in being upset that someone was accusing her of something she hadn't done. By the next weekend, Liz believed Cecelia, too. Both of the girls had become convinced that there was a ghost in their room. It went on for months. They were working together to arrange the fairies in ways they could remember to see how the ghost would move them. They even tried to spell words to communicate with it. They took pictures and showed me before and after shots of the *fairies lined up by size one day and switched around the next. The rest of us decided they had let their imaginations run amok, but it wasn't hurting anything.*

*And then Noah got caught. No one had suspected that either of the boys had any interest in playing with the fairies. They'd both mocked the collection enough that it seemed unlikely. Noah wasn't exactly playing with them though. He was sneaking into the girls' room only to move them a bit and see how long it took Liz to notice. He was nine. He thought it was hilarious when a ghost started getting the blame. I still cannot believe he had the patience to keep it going for as long as he did and that he could keep a straight face when the girls were inventing stories about why the ghost was haunting their room. Cecelia named it Muffy. My dad has joked that Noah was lucky we didn't all start calling him Muffy after that.*

*Noah has always been a prankster. That was one of his most memorable ones. I'm telling you about it so you'll understand why some of us are kicking ourselves for not suspecting him when the box disappeared. You remember the box? You can rest assured that it's been found. Here's what happened.*

*When Noah left that night, he took the box with him and stuck it in the back seat of Cecelia's car. She's been complaining about being forgetful because of what she calls pregnancy brain. He thought she would see the box when she left but not remember putting it out there, and it would mess with her head a bit. But it was dark when she left, and he put it on the floor and they already have a car seat back there and I don't know. Somehow neither Cecelia nor her husband noticed the box until they went back to the car for church on Sunday. At that point, she did suspect Noah. She called him to give him a piece of her mind, and that's when the rest of us found out. He didn't know she didn't see it right away and feels bad that Mom was freaking out and Dad was taking the heat. It all worked out, and I think even Cecelia will be laughing about it soon.*

*Tell me more about you. No siblings, but do you have much extended family? Do you cook? Do you keep your place tidy or don't worry as long as you can find what you need? What would you consider, hypothetically, a fair division of labor for spouses? When did you move out, and do you still have a good relationship with your parents? Do you consider yourself a private person? I don't want to come off as overly nosy, but we are trying to get to know each other and you said questions help. I'm looking forward to hearing from you again.*

> *Katie*

Katie turned off her computer. Even if Cameron saw the message right away, it would take him a few minutes to read it. She hoped he would take the time to write a lot, too. She checked her watch and vowed to wait a full twenty-four hours before she looked for a reply.

Unfortunately, that did not stop her from thinking about a reply. In her mind's eye, Cameron West was sitting at his desk smiling as he typed out a bunch of fun facts about himself. That was so wrong. Even if this online Cameron was the same guy, he wasn't at work at 7 o'clock on a Tuesday night. Katie's ideal match wouldn't be working so late or composing personal messages on work time. She didn't have any other settings in which to picture Cameron and shouldn't be picturing him at all. She prayed for a response that included an identifying feature, like really blond hair or an eyepatch.

The next day at work, Katie got an idea. First, she got a phone call. It was someone from another company asking when a particular invoice would be paid. That was what most of her work calls were about. Katie had some standard words about looking into it and nudging someone to get it approved, but they weren't just words. She quickly found the invoice in question. All but one of the charges had been matched up and were ready to be paid. She was mildly surprised to see the outstanding item was not one of Connie's files.

It was an older guy named Mike. He usually got back to her within a few hours, and it had been a few days.

Mike was in the same office as Connie. That was only part of Katie's idea. They both also shared an office with Cameron. If she brought something to ask Connie about, that would be an excuse to talk to Mike in person at the same time. And as long as she was there, maybe she could think of something to say to Cameron, something more than hello. Her idea was that while she was waiting to hear from online Cameron, she could try to get some information from the other one. Maybe it would be something that would help link or separate the guys.

Katie wrote file numbers and dollar amounts on sticky notes. She ran her fingers through her hair, then turned off her monitor to subtly check her reflection. She usually kept her hair behind her ears. With it forward, it didn't look better, it only looked as though she was trying to hide her ears. Why would she want to do that? She pushed it where it belonged and moved into the hallway.

That light was still flickering. Her boss's door was closed. There was no need to wave as she walked past. Her feet slowed as she approached Cameron's office. What if she found out he was the same person she'd been sending messages? It wouldn't be appropriate to talk about that at work. There would be nothing dishonest about waiting to break it to him online. He could end the budding connection quickly and impersonally. Everyone would be grateful to avoid having that level of awkwardness in an office.

She mashed her lips against the smile that wanted to break out when she saw Cameron. He had a phone pressed to his ear and an expression that suggested someone was giving him a long-winded answer.

"So... Friday?" he said into the phone. His eyes went to the ceiling as he listened to an answer that clearly had more words than simply yes or no.

Katie focused her attention on Connie. Her head was bent

forward so Katie could see the darker, graying roots in the otherwise blonde hair. One of Connie's hands was hovering over the desktop like a hammer ready to smack the first mole to pop while the other hand splayed fingers marking at least three different places in a stack of files. This would not be a good time to interrupt, but it never was.

It took Connie a few moments to notice Katie standing by her desk. When she glanced up, her elbows slumped to her sides. She frowned and said, "Do you need something?"

"I still have a few numbers that aren't lining up on my end," Katie said. "I wonder if you've had a chance to look at any of these files." She pressed one of her sticky notes to Connie's desk.

Connie hardly looked at the note. "I don't know," she said, turning away to examine the files between her fingers. "I have a million things to do today though. I'll have to get to your issues later."

"Okay. Let me know if you have questions about what I wrote."

Connie gave no indication that she was still listening. Katie only needed to be able to record the date she'd asked. An answer wasn't necessary. Eventually, if the bills became past due, Katie would need to go up the ladder for approval. She had to be able to show that she hadn't bothered the higher-ups first. She turned to Mike's desk. "Hey, Mike, do you have a minute?"

The older guy – she guessed sixtyish – sat back in his chair and gave her full eye contact. "Katherine," he said, sounding delighted, "to what do I owe the pleasure?"

She offered her most pleasant smile in return. "I got a call about one of yours. I sent you an email about it last Friday, but I haven't heard back so I thought I'd check in while I'm here."

"Oh, dear. I hope you aren't thinking I forgot about you." He leaned forward, grabbed his mouse and his mail appeared on the screen.

Katie averted her eyes for privacy's sake. Cameron's desk

faced Mike's. That was a nice place for her eyes to land. He was reading something on his screen while lightly tapping a pen against his desk. She watched his eyes dart side to side in tiny movements. They were light brown with a hint of yellow. Some might call that hazel. A romantic might even say it was a brown that had taken on the tint of old paper saved because of the cherished memories it held. Katie wasn't that sappy, or at least she was trying not to be that sappy. His hair was a more solid brown. He seemed to go a few months between haircuts, and it curled more when it covered more of his forehead as it did now. She didn't have any silly descriptions of his hair, only the more practical thought that perhaps the online Cameron would mention a haircut the same time she noticed this Cameron's hair get shorter. That might take a month, however, and would assume both that they were still in contact and that he felt a haircut worth mentioning.

"I'm sorry, Katherine. It looks like I *did* forget about you." Mike's voice brought her attention back to the closer desk. "Your note got buried under some abundant – but less important I assure you – messages. This is what you need?" He pointed to her message on his screen.

It matched the numbers on her sticky note. She set the note down. "Yeah, that's the one."

"Great." He tapped her note. "This'll save me from copying it down. I don't have enough information here to know why it's different so I'll have to dig up the file. I shouldn't have any trouble getting back to you before lunch though. Will that work?"

"That'll be wonderful. Thanks, Mike." She took a few slow steps before stopping again next to Cameron. "Hey, Cameron."

"Hi." His eyes came up for only a second, then moved back to her as he registered that she wasn't just passing by. "Am I in trouble, too?"

She smiled and hoped that was surprise and not apprehension she heard in his voice. "No," she said. "As a matter of fact, I was just thinking that you might be the only one here I've never had to ask for clarification."

"Oh." His eyes scanned the room, possibly for anyone obviously listening in. "I guess I've been lucky."

"Maybe," Katie said. "But I think there has to be a fair amount of diligence on your part, too. I should say thank you."

"Um… you're welcome?" He seemed to be questioning whether or not he needed to be thanked more than the appropriate response. Then he smiled somewhat mischievously and said, "I hope my streak isn't about to be ruined because you commented on it."

"That would be a shame." Katie was relieved that her laugh sounded less giggly than she felt. "I guess then you could at least blame me."

He nodded. "I hope we both remember that when you come in here complaining that something I did doesn't make sense."

"You have permission to remind me," she said. "Not that I'm admitting I go around complaining about things."

Cameron continued to smile, but his eyes lowered to the pen he was tapping against his desk again.

The pause was long enough that Katie felt it must be obvious she was reluctant to leave though she had nothing else to say. She needed to leave. "Have a good day," she said. She exited in a hurry, not even waiting for a response.

The hallway seemed somehow longer on the return trip. Katie was slightly flustered by the stiff end to what had been a mostly positive exchange. But she was quickly able to return to professional mode. The day passed with dispassionate numbers, reports and emails. It wasn't until she got home that she realized how stupid her idea had been.

How had she thought it would help? Had she expected him to see her and think, "You look like someone with no redheads in your immediate family, you must be the woman I met through Courting Catholics?" Or did she think she could tell by the way he held his pen that he was a guy who never played a game called Tichu? If she tried to talk to him again, she'd have to plan a specific connection to target. In the meantime, getting information from the online Cameron would be the more reasonable approach. Reasonable but frustrating. There was no message from him after a full day hiatus on checking.

5

It was a week before Katie got another message from Cameron. She did find a message from a different guy who appeared to be a poor match. She wondered if he had even read her profile. She also wondered how she would respond if she was contacted by someone at all promising while she still had hopes for Cameron. It wasn't a question of ethics but of sanity. Her thoughts were all over the place just with one possible match. In the week she didn't hear from him, she guessed that he was also trying to balance eager with overeager. She convinced herself he had lost interest. She fantasized about him taking so long because he was writing pages and pages in reply and agonizing over the wording of the thoughts he wanted to convey. She thought he might be experiencing a long-term highly localized power outage or connection failure. She wondered if a security issue had temporarily frozen his account. She'd even been briefly tempted to ask him if he'd sent a message that had been swallowed by a glitch.

And then she saw a message with his name on it. Before opening it, she took a few minutes to mentally prepare herself. She reminded herself that the budding relationship was barely a bud, certainly not big enough to put all her eggs in, even if he did want to continue. And if he didn't, the bud was too small to hurt when it was crushed. When she almost believed all that, she began to read.

Katie,

When you began by saying I'd given you a lot of material, I was afraid you were about to mock everything I'd said. I was glad you didn't mean that kind of material. I'm not even sure why I expected otherwise except that I guess I'm still a little apprehensive about all this. I'm also glad you don't sound in a hurry to meet in person. I like the anonymity for now.

But that doesn't mean I won't describe myself. Like you, I have brown hair and brown eyes. I'm a few inches taller. I can't say exactly how many since you couldn't say exactly how tall you are, which I thought was kind of odd. I'm probably fairly average. That's about it.

I can't tell you how relieved I was to hear that the box was found. That's only partially sarcastic. I don't think I could be Catholic and not be a big fan of tradition, even a somewhat frivolous one with a lowercase t. You described the situation in a way that I would have been surprised if it was really lost. Still definitely glad it resolved in an amusing way. I'd love to hear more stories of Noah's pranks.

I'm afraid I'm not the storyteller that you are, but something kind of funny happened this week. My friend Trevor apparently made a fool of himself in front of some girl. I shouldn't laugh at that, and I honestly feel bad for him. But the way he told us about it was just funny. He didn't want to talk about it and just kept slipping out stupid things he said. If I pieced it together correctly, his grandmother somehow convinced him to go to a furniture store for his morning coffee, without which he doesn't function well. There was a pretty girl there, and compounded with his groggy state, he said a lot of things he didn't mean to say and might have offended her. Something about her must have really made an impression though because it sounds like he's going to try to make it up to her.

You asked about my extended family and my relationship with my parents after I moved out, and that's actually all connected. I have quite a few cousins, but most of them are

39

girls or significantly older or younger than I am. Elijah is the only one I'm very close to, and he also happens to be my roommate. I lived at home while I was in school. Living on my own sounded kind of expensive, and my parents weren't in a hurry to get rid of me so I thought I would stay at home just through the summer and have a few full-time paychecks in the bank before I became an adult.

A few months before I graduated, however, the situation changed. My grandma, my mom's mom, moved in with us. I love my grandma. We all love her. But the transition was a little rocky. She didn't want to be a burden and tried to help out a lot. My mom didn't like sharing the kitchen and seemed to take any cleaning her mom did as a criticism of her housekeeping skills. There was some tension.

Elijah is only a year older than me, but he didn't go to college (well, he went for one semester) so he had been on his own for a few years. I asked him how he was managing or if he had any advice. He told me that he wasn't having any trouble paying the bills, but that it was difficult to get any savings built up. He confessed that he'd been thinking about getting a roommate for some time but that he didn't think he would be able to find one who would leave him alone. I was like, yes, I would like a roommate who pays part of the rent and otherwise ignores me, too. We found a two-bedroom for only a little more than what Elijah was paying, which split in half would be a good deal for both of us. We moved in only a few weeks after I graduated.

Meanwhile, my mom and grandma have made peace. I don't know what the chore list looks like, but I know that my mom cooks during the week and my grandma cooks on weekends. That's important so I know who I'm complimenting when I eat there. And it brings me to your question about a fair division of household labor. I don't think it's a cop-out to say there is no right answer. What is fair is whatever each household has agreed upon. For example, if I could count ten chores that I was doing and my wife handled one, but it was the one I most hated (I'll give you a hint: it's cooking.) then

*I'd probably consider that fair. Circumstances matter. If one spouse is spending more time at home, then it might make sense for that spouse to do more of the work around the house. Although, for the record, I think the kids should also be expected to help, within reason. The chores might also need to be redistributed from time to time, maybe as there are more kids or the kids get older. I hope enough communication would keep it fair. Does that sound cliché? Everyone says communication is important in marriages, yet lots of couples struggle with it.*

*Back to that aside about me hating cooking. I need to be honest that the woman who marries me, if she exists, should not expect much help in the kitchen. Cooking makes me feel like a failure. My mom did all the cooking when I was growing up and never tried to teach me. I thought I could just figure it out on my own. Recipes generally have pretty clear instructions. I like to think I'm a fairly intelligent person. I can follow directions. But I set off the smoke detector on a few early attempts and got glass in my foot after I broke a bowl on the floor and it just feels like way too much effort for the payoff of having something to eat when there are lots of things to eat without the effort. Perhaps I would hate it less if I practiced more. But for now, I'm eating a lot of sandwiches (Hence the need for mustard. BTW, have you ever actually tried it? What's not to like?) and occasionally inviting myself to my parents' house for dinner.*

*I think I have several second favorite games. Is that allowed? There are many good ones, but Tichu is in a class by itself. I have to say I was impressed that your questions about it show you have extensive gaming experience. Tichu has cards numbered two through ace like a standard deck but with different suits and a few special cards. It's a trick-taking game. You don't play one card at a time though but any of several combinations of cards. Those can only be beaten by the same combination with higher cards. That might not be an awesome description. It's difficult to explain without examples in front of me.*

*What do I want to know about you? What about your favorite or second favorite game? Are you more of a homebody or do you only play games when there's nothing more fun to do? You mentioned paying for experiences. Do you have plans to travel or a bucket list of places to see? Do you have allergies or disabilities or I'm not sure what I'm trying to ask? I guess is there something about you that someone in your life should be aware of in order to keep you comfortable? How do you feel about nature? Do you ever go camping or fishing, things like that? Can you tell that I don't know what to ask? I think too often we don't know what will cause disagreements until we're already disagreeing. Should I ask about politics to get the ball rolling? I was about to write, don't answer that, but now actually seems like a better time to talk about it than later. I think that says I only want you to answer if you'll say things I like. I'm not sure I should admit that. It sounds selfish.*

*Well, whatever you want to tell me will be good to know, and I have a feeling it will be entertaining as well.*
   *Cameron*

     Three days or only two this time? Katie deliberated how long to pause. Regardless how long she waited to send her next message, Katie couldn't think of a reason she shouldn't start writing it. She assured him that he didn't sound selfish for wanting to avoid conflict and division. She pointed out that the faith questions touched on a few important issues, and if faith continued to be their guide they might not disagree on anything huge. She listed a few games she liked and said a night in usually sounded better than a night out. She told him she laughed at the crack about her not knowing her own height, and that she was reasonably sure she hadn't grown since she was last measured, just hadn't given it much thought. Katie admitted she preferred modern comforts over camping, but she enjoyed hiking and using leaves and flowers in some craft projects. She told him about the time Noah got up early and changed Michael's clock so he'd think he overslept and the time he switched all the cereal bags around inside the boxes. It ended up being her longest letter yet.

Cameron responded in kind, and quickly. He said he'd been praying and felt more confident that Katie was a connection he wanted to pursue. He was in until or unless one of them had a good reason to stop writing. The best part was a funny story about fishing with his dad. Cameron said he didn't particularly like fishing but went occasionally to spend time with his dad. They once spent nearly three hours in the rain. Cameron had been a teenager and completely miserable at the time. After a few years though, he could laugh at the way his dad had spent the entire time insisting that it would stop raining any minute.

He asked the following evening if Katie was available for a real-time exchange. They spent nearly two hours sending brief messages back and forth. Everything he said made her want to ask another question, and he appeared equally curious. Katie eventually suggested she needed a break to compose thoughts on the things left unanswered. Cameron agreed and said it was getting late anyway. When she was convinced he'd signed off, she typed out one last message, something she hadn't wanted answered in a rush.

> **Cameron,**
> **Here's one more question I'd love you to address in your next note. Why are you here? It's probably obvious that I joined the site because I'm thirty, the whole biological clock thing is real. But you're younger, and male. Was it a whim? Were you just being impatient or was it something else?**
> **Katie**

She took a book to the bedroom with her. Reading for a few minutes usually cleared her head and made her drowsy. It was difficult to settle her mind enough to focus on the words at first. She had considered asking Cameron where he worked. The simple question could solve her more pressing question. It was specific though. He had said he preferred the anonymity for a while, and so did Katie. Asking would have opened the door for more specifics, maybe a picture or even a meeting. Katie did want that eventually, but she was afraid. The more they found in common, the more likely a rejection would be based on him not finding her physically attractive. That would hurt.

Katie finally began to read. The topic was resting in the presence of God. She felt calmed and drifted into a peaceful sleep. The peace only lasted until morning. She hadn't even finished breakfast when memories of the chat with Cameron flooded her mind along with images of the other Cameron. That wasn't right. She had to separate them. But that would have to wait.

Cameron had said he planned to avoid sending messages on weekday mornings lest he end up making himself late for work. The responsible side of that sentiment was admirable and the other part was flattering. Katie would also be tempted to spend too much time on a message if she started writing one. Her mornings were tightly scheduled. Breakfast, prayer, shower, update to-do lists, go to work.

The early part of Katie's workday was fuller than usual as two people were out sick. Shortly after lunch, her boss entered the room. He approached one of the empty desks and rifled through a few papers on the corner. Then he went to the other one and stood with his hands on his hips, frowning at it.

He was probably making sure the three remaining employees weren't letting the work pile up. On the one hand, that was his job. On the other, Katie knew he wouldn't help if they were falling behind. He would only tell them too late not to fall behind. He wasn't a terrible boss, just not very proactive. And he was a big guy with a loud voice that sounded angry even when he wasn't.

Katie had mostly gotten used to him, but she still hesitated to draw his attention. It didn't appear anyone else was going to say anything. "Is there something we can help you find?" she asked.

He grunted. Then he shook his head and said, "You're doing a good job," before he left.

"Someone's in a good mood today," one of her coworkers observed.

Katie smiled agreement. He had sounded a bit less gruff. She knew he meant his "good job" in the generic, adequate sense and that it was directed to the room at large, but she still lapped up whatever praise she could get. It made her wonder if she could ask Cameron how he felt about his boss without mentioning names. She hardly knew the manager of his department though. His answer would be unlikely to include a recognizable trait.

There she was confusing the two guys again. Katie sighed at herself and concentrated on her work. Until she encountered a rather interesting number, $112.32. That was an expected payout. The amount on the invoice, however, was $112.23. The mildly interesting thing about the number was that it actually fell within her extremely limited purview. After five years with the company, Katie had been granted permission to correct any payouts within a dollar without seeking approval. If this had been real authority, she'd wish she could say it was a result of her proven record and some sort of promotion. It happened only after another employee begged management to let everyone round off their payouts. No one else took advantage, but Katie and the other accounts payable grunts could use the blanket permission to fix typos in the cents column. Katie had let her siblings tease her about all the power going to her head.

But she was tempted not to use that power this time. It was Cameron who had swapped the numbers. That made the situation a bit more thought-provoking. Should she really go and bug him when she didn't need to?

Katie hadn't answered the question before she was already in the hallway, which was what told her it might be a bad idea. She turned around under that dying light, then stopped. There was no one around. There were muffled voices from various directions. Her shadow flashed on the wall while thoughts flashed through her head.

The dominant idea was that she wasn't trying to fan the flames of a crush, she was trying to find the truth of the situation.

Katie reset her steps towards that big office. This time when her eyes sought Cameron, she didn't feel guilty or immature. She was doing her job. Sort of. His head was bent over his work, and he pushed some hair off his forehead as he glanced up. Her legs became slightly rubbery, but her mind stayed clear.

"Hi, Katherine," he said. "Are you looking at me today?"

She looked at him every day, but she knew he was asking if her question was for him. "I'm afraid so." She stuck her sticky note to his desk. "This is the file. Nine cents isn't worth looking it up if you don't have time. But after I just commented on how you never make mistakes, I couldn't resist finding out if it was you or whoever billed us."

"You came in here to rub my nose in nine cents?" He was laughing.

"No," she said, glad he was amused. "It's entirely possible the mistake is on the other end. I was honestly curious."

"I'll check and send you an email. But remember whose fault it is if I messed up."

She nodded. At his comment and then towards the window on the other side of his desk. "Clouds are still gathering. I hope the rain holds off until after we get home."

"Or passes quickly," he said.

They shared a smile over the sentiment while Katie laughed at herself. What had she expected her statement on the weather would prompt him to say? By the way, I've never been fishing in the rain? That wasn't just unlikely, it was downright absurd. And she was out of things to say. "Well, let me know."

He picked up her sticky note as she left, apparently moving her frivolous request to the top of his workload. That shouldn't cause her anything but remorse over wasting his time. But her pulse stayed high as she returned to her own desk.

The guy sounded promising. Katie skimmed her eyes over the profile again, torn between curiosity and annoyance. She had two messages, one from Cameron and one from this new guy named Anthony. She had forced herself to read Anthony's message first, told herself it would be quick to find out why he was wrong for her and politely let him know.

But nothing jumped out as wrong. He answered all the faith questions the same and was only two years younger. If the picture hadn't been touched, he was fairly nice looking, too. He did live at least an hour's drive away. That would be doable, especially if they met somewhere in the middle. Katie would want to know more about Anthony if she wasn't dying to know what Cameron wrote in his latest message. It wouldn't be wise to ignore one potential match for another. She typed up an invitation for Anthony to tell her more about himself and tried to ignore the feeling that she hoped he'd admit something that ruled him out. Then she opened the message from Cameron.

> *Katie,*
> *Why am I here? That's a philosophical question that the Church answers concisely with to know God, to love God and to serve God. I know you meant more specifically here. I wish my answer could be as simple and beautiful, but it's*

*awkward and humiliating. I did say that honesty is important though so here goes.*

*I worked at a fast-food place when I was in high school and most of college. I met a girl there. Her name was Isabelle. She was in 11th grade, and I was in 12th. We went out a couple of times, and she quickly became my girlfriend. Or so I thought. We dated over a year. Sort of. It seemed that she usually had to work the nights I didn't so we didn't spend nearly as much time together as I would have liked. She was very different, mostly raised by her mom, an atheist. She had a stepdad who dropped out of her life shortly before we met and a pair of former stepsisters she was secretly still in contact with because she wasn't supposed to talk to them.*

*Anyway, she seemed broken somehow, kind of angry at life but very pretty. She always seemed interested in everything I had to say about Christianity and being Catholic. I thought I might be gradually converting her. I heard occasional rumors from other people we worked with that she was dating other guys. I dismissed it as sour grapes. I thought she was better looking than me so people just didn't understand how I got so lucky.*

*One day a coworker pulled me aside to tell me specifically that her brother had been out with Isabelle the previous night and came home laughing at how she'd told him about some goody-goody from work who thought she was his girlfriend. I checked the work schedule, something I had never done when she told me she had to work because I trusted her. I thought checking the schedule would only confirm she hadn't been with the other guy. But she wasn't on the schedule.*

*When I asked her, she immediately started laughing. She said it was about time I stopped being so gullible because she didn't know how much longer she could keep up the act. Then she thanked me for the "free stuff" and hung up. Word spread quickly. Over the next few days, several of the other employees shared with me how she'd been mocking me behind my back. I think they thought that would make me feel better about the breakup. It only made me realize how many people had been laughing at or pitying me for months. At least.*

*I didn't quit. That's probably the only part of the whole fiasco I can look back on with anything less than horror. It was awful for a while, but it did get better, and I didn't let her take my job, too. There are the gory details. The lesson, after some time and reflection, was that I never really tried to know her. I only loved who I wanted her to be or who I hoped she was. There were so many times in hindsight where I could see that I told myself she hadn't meant something the way it sounded or that she was only joking.*

*That's why I'm here, to more objectively evaluate a possible relationship. No chance of being blinded by a pretty face when you won't show me a picture. But seriously, this setting encourages both of us to look at what's most important first. I don't want to get to a point where I already want to avoid a breakup before I'm "allowed" to ask if someone wants kids or has a good relationship with Jesus or has a boatload of debt. You don't have a boatload of debt, do you?*

*Let's forget about all that. You definitely don't need to comment on it. To help us move on, I'll tell you what happened on Friday. It was Tichu night, of course. When I went to start my car, the battery was dead. Elijah doesn't get up until about ten so getting him up at seven would be kind of like the middle of the night for him. I went next door first. There's an older guy over there I know a little, but he didn't seem to be home. I didn't want to bum a favor off someone I've never talked to so I went in and knocked on Elijah's door.*

*It is not easy to wake him up. Eventually, I was able to explain the situation and get him outside. As I opened my trunk for the jumper cables, I remembered loaning them to someone at work several months ago. I never got them back. Elijah said he didn't know if he had any. He didn't. We couldn't find any in his car either. He told me that if I could* find some cables, I was welcome to use his car. Then he handed me his keys and went back to bed.

I was tempted to just stand in the street with the hood up to see how long it took for someone to stop and offer to help. But it was pretty quiet – we live on a dead end street – and the guys were already waiting on me. I realized I should have asked Elijah if I could borrow his car, but I couldn't take it without asking or wake him up again. I called my parents. I was sure one of them would be willing to help. Now you can probably tell I was already getting frustrated when I had what turned out to be a very annoying conversation with my mom.

My dad was doing a men's retreat weekend and had already left for that. My mom and grandma had decided that with him out of the house, they would do some sort of weird girl stuff. She told me she was in the middle of something called a mud mask and wasn't fit to leave the house. I told her she wouldn't have to get out of the car at all, but she didn't want anyone to see her through the windows. So I asked if I walked over there – they only live about a half mile away – could I take her jumper cables to use on Elijah's car. Then she insisted that I should take her car and use it instead. When I pointed out that her car would be stuck at my house – or I'd have to drive it back and walk again – she offered to ride with me to drive it back. I said if she was willing to ride with me, why couldn't she just drive over here? She laughed as she realized the flawed logic, and I thought she was about to agree. Instead, she said, "You're right. Just keep my car, and we'll figure out how to get it in the morning."

I had already started walking while we talked, and it occurred to me that Trevor and Ryan don't live that much farther away. I told my mom I'd just walk there and deal with the car in the morning. Maybe I could borrow jumper cables while I was there. I texted Trevor to let him know I'd be late. Then I noticed the wind picking up and dark clouds moving in. You know how those summer storms are. I knew it was going to roll in and pour on me, and roll out again before I could get there. It didn't even seem worth trying to jog. It kind of *made me laugh though. Sometimes when things start to pile up, laughing is the only way to go.*

*But barely a minute later, Ryan showed up to give me a ride. He volunteered to stop by in the morning to jump my car and said he would follow me to get a new battery, just in case. The night continued to improve as we still had time to play two games of Tichu, and I won both. It wasn't Ryan's best night because not only did he lose both games but now I know who to call first next time I have a problem.*

*I guess I've postponed the answer to whether or not I'm a slob long enough and will finally come clean. Wait, looks like I had one more bad pun. The real reason I keep avoiding the question is that I know people have very different standards. I think I keep the place pretty clean, but I can imagine you seeing it and saying, "You call this clean?" Or at least I could if I knew what you look like. Still not ready to share a picture?*
    *Cameron*

She wasn't. Katie feared sharing a picture more now than when she was looking at that one of her biting her glasses. Meeting someone online was supposed to rearrange the emotional part of the process. It was supposed to let her evaluate a guy objectively and see if some heart flutters could develop from there, not the other way around. Cameron had, using different words, described it exactly the same way. That could be more evidence that they were a good match. But Katie was much more emotional than she anticipated. She was terrified to take the next step before she divided the real Cameron from the Cameron at work. Meeting him would do that, but she wanted to do it first. And the irrationality of that meant she was seriously emotional.

Katie pushed the computer aside, wanting some time with her thoughts before she wrote any out to Cameron. Instead, she was distracted by a call from Liz.

"Hey, Katie. You busy?"

"I always have time to talk to one of my favorite sisters."

"Funny," Liz said dryly. "Are you going to Mom and Dad's on Saturday?"

Their mom had sent an invitation to all her kids by group text earlier in the day. Katie had replied to everyone that she would be there. "Yes," she said, waiting for the real question.

"Have you talked to Cecelia?"

"About going to Mom and Dad's?" Katie was confused because Cecelia had also confirmed she would be there.

"Just in general," Liz said.

"Have I talked to her in general? Uh... I think she did call me once since we were all together last," Katie said. "Is there something specific I was supposed to have talked to her about?"

Liz chuckled into the phone. "Well, I don't know if I should get in the middle."

"In the middle of what?"

"Hmm." There was a brief pause. Katie pictured Liz shifting the phone to her other ear, something she always seemed to do when she changed topics. It was a weird habit Katie had noticed when they were both still teenagers. "Cecelia is afraid of you right now. She's been trying to make her baby's angel and failing. She doesn't want Mom to know she's messed up and wasted some of the supplies, and she thinks you're going to yell at her and refuse to help after all the fuss she made about you not being the one to make her angel."

"Oh, my goodness." Katie laughed.

"See, this is why I called," Liz said. "You can get the laugh out of the way now and not laugh when you talk to Cecelia."

Katie had mostly gotten it out of her system. "I don't know," she said. "I might still have to laugh. She was so mad when she thought the box was lost, and she told me I wouldn't be allowed anywhere near it again unless I had a baby of my own. And now she wants my help?"

"I'm sorry." Liz sounded suddenly more serious. "I didn't know she said that."

Katie took a breath. She had tried to joke about not being allowed near the box, but the longing for a baby of her own was painful. The fact that Liz recognized it made it difficult to gloss over. "Don't worry," she said. "Cecelia gets to blame everything on pregnancy hormones right now."

"So… any luck on the internet dating?"

Katie sighed at the unsurprising transition. She had admitted to her family that she'd decided to give the site a try. But she was clear that she wasn't going to talk about it further unless there was something to tell. Bringing it up at this point in the conversation made it sound like a desperate bid to have a child before she was too old and not simply being proactive in going after the family she wanted. Liz must be able to see that so it made Katie even less interested in discussing it than otherwise. "No," she said simply.

"None at all?" Liz sounded skeptical. "Surely you've gotten some nibbles."

"I'm not a fish."

Liz laughed. "It's the fish who nibble."

Katie found herself smiling. Her mood lightened as she accused her sister of calling her a worm.

"If the shoe fits," Liz said.

Then they both laughed at trying to put a shoe on a worm.

"Okay," Katie said. "I'll tell you that I have exchanged messages with a few guys, but I have nothing beyond that to report."

"Anyone local?" Liz asked.

"I have nothing beyond that to report."

"No. Be gentle." The faded quality of her voice would have made it obvious she was talking to one of her kids even if the words hadn't. Then Liz was back. "I need to put people to bed in a minute. Are you gonna help Cecelia or give her a hard time?"

"Maybe both," Katie said.

Liz laughed and said, "Be nice," before she hung up.

If Cecelia was worrying about asking for help, it would be a kindness to talk to her sooner rather than later. Katie would be kind. But she would still act like a sibling. Katie's other sister answered her phone immediately and sounded cheery. "Hi, Katie."

"Cecelia. How're you feeling?"

"Great, actually," Cecelia said. "I had a power nap when I got home from work. When I woke up, the little one was kicking like crazy, and I just enjoyed that for a while."

Katie smiled at the contented tone. It faded when Cecelia immediately followed it with a question about how the internet dating was going. Was that the most interesting thing about her now? "It's fine," she said.

"Define fine."

"Okay."

"No, have you connected with anyone with potential? How many guys have messaged you? Oh, and what picture did you use?"

"What part of I don't want to give details until or unless there's something specific to share is difficult for people to understand?"

"All of it," Cecelia said. "We want to groan with you over the losers and help you sort through the good guys so we can root for the best one."

"You make it sound like some sort of sporting event."

"Huh." Cecelia laughed. "It did sort of. But I'm just trying to say that a loving family wants to be involved in your life."

"And if I'm ever *involved* with a guy, I'll tell you."

"Come on. It's been at least a month, right? You must have something to tell."

"Not really," Katie said. It was time to turn the conversation around. "What's going on on your end of the phone?"

"Not much." There was a pause as Cecelia drew in some air.

Katie wondered if she was thinking of another angle to try to pry information or thinking of the favor Liz thought she wanted to ask. She would wait patiently.

"I... uh, we picked out a crib."

"Yeah. You already told me about that."

"Oh, right. And I'll see you at Mom and Dad's in a few days?"

"Yeah," Katie said. It had sounded like a question even though they both knew the answer. Cecelia seemed to be trying to think of something to say. Since she always had things to say, it was likely she was thinking of something she didn't want to say. Katie remembered her thought to be kind and nudged her that direction. "Have you finished the ornament for your baby?"

"Uh... no."

"Have you started it?"

"I... uh, sort of."

"Sort of?" This was taking a lot of nudges.

"Well, I started it more than once. The pattern is... not as clear as... I've had a bit of trouble." Cecelia appeared to be creating an opening for an offer of help rather than making the request.

Katie wasn't going to make it that easy. "What kind of trouble?" she asked.

"Just... some... well, I know you've seen Mom's pattern."

"Uh-huh."

"You didn't think it was difficult to follow at all?"

"Not really," Katie said. "Though I did watch Mom make the one for Noah. That might have helped."

"Yeah. That probably was... good."

Katie had probably stalled enough. "Liz told me you might want some help."

"You talked to Liz?" Cecelia made a noise between a sigh and a grumble. "All right. How much crow do I have to eat to get you to come over and help me? The material for the wings frays and falls apart when I try to cut it. The head had all kinds of weird wrinkles when I tried to glue on the cloth. The marker bled so bad the eyes are ginormous, and I cut the dress too small so I have to redo all the cross-stitching, which was the one part I actually got right."

"That's enough," Katie said. "I only wanted you to admit you want my help. How about you bring the box with you to Mom and Dad's? I'll help you there."

"I'd rather not take the box out of my house and risk losing it again."

"You mean you don't want everyone else to know that you need help?"

"Uh… that, too." Cecelia's voice was remorseful.

"I could point out that the box was actually at your house the whole time it was lost."

"And I could point out that Noah is not funny," Cecelia said. "And that you said you were letting me off the hook."

"All right." Katie and her sister agreed on an earlier time to work together. She ended the call feeling that it was nice to be needed. And that she would enjoy sharing the latest development with Cameron.

7

The idea was beyond ridiculous. Katie didn't seriously consider it. She only amused herself with thoughts of wandering the building asking if anyone had forgotten to return a set of jumper cables. People would think she was nuts. Unless she actually found someone, then he'd wonder how she knew. Cameron would hear about it, and if there was anything to figure out, he would figure it out before she did. That thought was less amusing.

She continued to exchange messages with that other Cameron, if it was another Cameron. Part of her enjoyed the mystery, and part of her was anxious to end it. And then Cameron – the one she was messaging – provided her with a possible solution.

She'd gotten him to give more details on some of his cooking disasters. To prove she didn't judge him too harshly, she admitted she'd once tried to make a pot pie without a recipe and ended up with undercooked chicken and a crust that was soggy on the bottom and slightly charred on the top. Cameron had, in only partial seriousness, listed the different sandwiches he could make without cooking if anyone ever wanted him to help feed a family. One of his favorites, a BLT, did require cooking though. He said that wasn't a problem because he knew a place that made an awesome one, and he'd just happened to have had it for lunch that day.

Katie thought his list of sandwiches and descriptions was funny. He related the importance of ingredient order for structural integrity and insisted a different flavor of mustard was all it took to make a completely different sandwich. The best part though, the part that really made her smile, was that he wrote the name of the restaurant where he liked the BLT. The January Café. Katie read the letter twice, as usual. On the third time through, she stopped at those words and considered if it might be the hint she needed.

She looked up the January Café. It was only ten minutes from work. She could go there for lunch. Cameron hadn't said anything about how often he went there, but he had said the sandwich was a favorite. How long would he wait before he treated himself again? A few weeks? Could she hold Cameron off on exchanging pictures that long?

The plan had a lot of holes in it, so many that it was more of a vague idea than a plan. Katie was going to have lunch at the January Café the very next day. It seemed unlikely that Cameron would be there twice in a row, and she wanted to scope out the place without worrying that she might unknowingly bump into him.

Katie had lunch at home most days. That was about ten minutes in the opposite direction. The timing wouldn't be difficult. It was nice to step out of the office for her break. She didn't socialize much at work. There were plenty of people with whom she was friendly. She got greetings with small talk and smiles, but there wasn't anyone she wanted to sit and talk with for an hour. Other than Cameron, which was a bad idea for different reasons. With anyone else, Katie would be tempted to return to her desk early.

The January Café was easy to find. Katie made only one turn after entering town. The street was fairly full, but there was a small parking lot not far from the restaurant. She stopped and backtracked on foot.

Her lunchtime was a bit earlier than average so she wasn't surprised to find the inside somewhat quiet. Only three tables had patrons. There were only two visible employees, marked by black aprons bearing a white logo. One, a middle-aged woman chatting with a customer, gave no indication that she noticed Katie. The other was a man behind a long counter in the back. He smiled and gestured towards the row of chairs in front of him, then to the many empty places. It was a clear sign that she was welcome to sit wherever she liked.

Katie chose a booth in the back left corner. From there, she had an excellent line of sight to the front door. She was also far enough away from it to not be the first person anyone entering would see, particularly if the place was a bit more crowded. She noticed a few menus at the edge of the table and pulled one in front of her.

The man who had been behind the counter stepped to her side a moment later. "Welcome to the January Café," he said. "Do you have any questions I can answer or would you just like a minute to look over the menu?" He seemed to recognize that she was a new or at least not recent customer.

"I would like a minute, thanks."

He nodded and moved away without another word.

Katie turned to the sandwich section of the menu and found the description for the BLT. Mustard? Wasn't mayo the customary dressing? This one did have mayo but also a honey Dijon mustard. She doubted either of those adjectives would cancel out the slightly sour, slightly bitter taste that made her tongue revolt. But she had no intention of ordering a BLT now anyway. If she ever came with Cameron, she'd try one out of curiosity, or perhaps a bite of his. For now, she would begin a search for her own favorite.

It only took a few visits for Katie to settle on the taco salad as her standard order. It had a strong flavor without being overly spicy and enough lettuce and tomato to be a real salad and not just a crushed taco trying to sound healthy. She enjoyed the atmosphere of the restaurant as much as the food. It was calm and somehow peaceful even with the friendly chatter that occasionally bounced between tables. The place had a core lunch crowd that was there nearly every day Katie was there. Even though she always brought a book and had only exchanged smiles of acknowledgement, she felt an almost unexplainable sense of belonging.

One Friday after she'd been there at least a dozen times, she got held up at work and came later than usual. The place was fairly full, and yet her corner spot was still open as though everyone had saved it for her. Katie slid into the booth and gave her standard order to Audra, a friendly blonde who had been bringing her a taco salad ever since she decided on it. Katie had read her nametag so many times it was hard not to think of her by name whether they really knew each other or not.

She opened her book while she waited for her food. She was taking a fiction break but had just started a new one and wasn't sucked into the plot yet. It was too easy for her mind to wander. Katie had run through countless scenarios in her head, and she didn't know where to bank her hopes. Every time the door opened, her eyes sought out a man who might be twenty-four years old, who had brown hair, and who liked sandwiches and worried about the best way to share his faith with the kids he didn't yet have. Would she recognize him? And what would she do if she did?

So far, the door had given her nothing but disappointment. Katie had thought Cameron's description was pretty generic, and yet she had enough information to rule out nearly everyone who entered the January Café. Most of the guys were too old. Some came in with families. There had been only two real possibilities. One guy who appeared to match the physical characteristics came in with a couple other guys, and they were all wearing orange vests and dirty boots. Though she still knew few details about Cameron's job, she knew it wasn't outside so that could not have been him. The other possibility was a young man who also appeared to arrive with coworkers, coworkers dressed for office jobs. The group was there regularly and sat at a fairly close table. Katie had tensely eavesdropped until she eventually heard someone calling him a different name.

Every time someone who was obviously not Cameron entered, she tried to picture what would happen if it could be him. Would she try to say something? Would she wait until she was home and ask in a message what he'd had for lunch that day? Would she want to talk and be too tongue-tied?

His messages had begun to hint at wanting to meet or at least try a phone call. He wasn't insistent, and they joked about who was more nervous. She wanted to meet him, but she was being stubborn about wanting to see him first. She had no face to insert in her scenarios, and that made every attempt morph into Cameron West. She needed to separate him before she could move forward with the real Cameron. Maybe. She felt certain it wasn't him yet it seemed important to prove that.

"Hi. No hurry with this." Audra set the check on the edge of the table.

Katie hadn't even realized she'd finished her salad yet.

"Forgive me if I'm out of line," Audra continued, "but I couldn't help noticing that you've been watching the door, and I wondered if there's anything I could help you with. I mean, I'm here a lot so maybe..." The offer trailed off but seemed sincere despite the indistinctness.

Katie was caught off guard. "You can tell I'm watching for someone?"

Audra nodded. Her eyes were compassionate. "But it's my job to pay attention to customers to see when they might need me. I'm sure no one else noticed."

That actually made sense. Audra sounded interested in helping, but Katie knew she couldn't. "I'm just hoping to solve a little mystery," she said.

"A mystery?" Audra's eyes glittered with much more interest.

Katie hadn't intended to tease her. The situation was probably beyond anyone's help. Except God's, of course. She took out her credit card so Audra could do her real job.

"Okay," she said as she took it. "I'll be right back."

There had been obvious disappointment in her voice, though she had tried to hide it. It made Katie smile to think the story could earn a connection if she wasn't too embarrassed to tell it.

She returned to work. When she passed Cameron's desk later, she didn't say much more than hello. She kept her silly thoughts about asking if he believed honey or Dijon would improve mustard to herself.

The other Cameron would get it. They'd had a playful argument about those adjectives, including whether or not honey was actually bee barf. Most of their communication had turned into short, quick exchanges in the evenings. But Friday was his Tichu night. Katie was thinking of that as she sat down to write a longer note.

*Hi Cameron,*
*How's the game going tonight? Or maybe I should ask how it went since you'll be finished by the time you're reading this. It's difficult to imagine since I still haven't seen any pictures of the cards. Thank you for challenging my self-control. Yes, that's sarcastic. I think it'd actually be easier to not look if it was something more important.*

*Cecelia's ornament is finally finished. I'm not at all worried about keeping my mouth shut about the name they picked for the baby. I didn't need her to swear me to secrecy. It only took three trips to her house, though it feels like more because of the extra phone calls talking her through a few things. Despite her trouble, I think she's even more adamant than ever that everyone else needs to make their own angels, too. I don't know if she feels that if she can learn then others can, too. Or if she wants them to have to learn because she did. But I know Michael doesn't want to so I'm afraid that will be the next bit of drama about the box. Cecelia will stubbornly pass it to him. I hope he will quietly give it to me so I can make the angel without mentioning it to anyone. With the baby coming in January, they won't need it until next*

*Christmas. We have tons of time to let people forget. I will not be surprised, however, if Michael tells her she's being stupid as he gives me the box right in front of her. That would be fun.*

*I finished a book recently that talked about how you address God when you pray and how it might affect your prayer life. I'm still trying to wrap my head around it. It asked you to consider whether you most commonly address God as God or Jesus or Lord or... God does have a lot of titles. Plus, it might mean you were addressing a specific person of God more than the others. This wasn't a psychological analysis of what it might say about you but an invitation to think about your relationship based on the title you are most comfortable with. It asked you to consider how your relationship might deepen if you spoke to one of the persons you unintentionally neglect. I found it all very thought-provoking, but I haven't come to any serious revelations or conclusions.*

*I have, on a completely unrelated and lighter note, come to a conclusion about my new favorite restaurant. It's the music, or rather the lack of music. I had lunch there again today, and I was thinking about the fact that it isn't particularly quiet. There are enough people around that there are voices and laughter and chairs scraping the ground and... you know, the noises people make. I've tried to do my lunch out before and usually felt I'd rather be at home where it's quiet, even at relatively empty restaurants. I thought maybe it's because I have a big family that people were easy to ignore. But I think it's because I'm supposed to ignore them. The conversations at other tables are none of my business. Whereas when someplace is piping music into my ears, I feel as though I'm supposed to be listening to the music that is often bland or awful.*

*Now I have a new puzzle. I've always thought I liked music. Am I much pickier than I thought or am I resentful about the fact that someone else picked it out for me? It might be both, and that isn't a puzzle I'll spend much time thinking about.*

*How's your puzzle coming? I know you said you don't care about the picture, but I hope it will be nice to look at. Some people do puzzles that are just one solid color for an extra challenge. I don't understand that. It's kind of like skipping the reward. I'd like to hear more about if your guesses are still plausible. And, of course, I want to hear more about anything else you'd like to tell me.*

    **Katie**

8

Cameron hadn't given any indication about whether or not he picked up on the hint. He laughed with Katie about the possibility of having to defend her ability to make Christmas ornaments. He described the picture he was building with jigsaw pieces as either an animal or some sort of furry planet. He thought it was looking very round and seemed to have only sky for background. He let her know that Tichu was in fact very important. She was smiling through most of his letter. He responded to most of what she'd written and added a few topics and questions of his own.

There wasn't a word about Katie's new favorite restaurant all weekend. It had been long enough since he mentioned the January Café by name that she hadn't really expected him to make the connection. It was intentionally subtle because part of her didn't want him to guess. She was getting impatient to meet him, but not so impatient that she was ready to suggest a specific time and place. Katie was just plain afraid, too afraid to think about why.

If Cameron had commented on her music pickiness or asked what she liked to eat there or made any mention at all, she probably would have assumed he missed the hint. The silence made her wonder. Did he recognize a place with lots of chattering and no music? Was he saying nothing to try to spot her there? Did he think if he asked if it was the January Café she would chicken out and stop eating there? Because she might.

Katie was still stuck in her wondering. She was looking at the door more often than before and looking at the pages of her book less than before. There was a bit of progress with one relationship though. Audra apologized for getting nosy without at least asking her name first. Katie introduced herself, and they began to exchange more friendly banter than simply placing and delivering an order. The January Café was a family business. Audra was also an artist and had work on display in the neighboring shop. If Katie came for a meal without the constraints of a work break, she wanted to check out the paintings. Audra teased her about being bold on a day she asked for something else.

Katie hadn't felt bold. She was just hungrier than normal. She'd skipped breakfast after having a rough night. She had talked to Cameron, really talked, actually heard his voice through a phone. It had been a short call because they had agreed to a time limit beforehand in an attempt to lessen nerves. They mostly reiterated a few things from recent messages. There was nothing distinctive in his voice – like an accent, an accent would have been nice – to distinguish him from Cameron West. She had never talked to that other Cameron on the phone to know his voice. There was no way to be sure that it was or wasn't him. Sleep was delayed while she fretted over the possibility that her own voice was more recognizable.

It was a possibility she needed to explore. As soon as Connie gave her an excuse, Katie walked down the flashy hallway of doom. Well, maybe doom was overly dramatic, but her heart raced – in a fearful way – at the idea of sensing recognition in Cameron's eyes. She kept her own eyes trained on Connie as she entered, then had the necessary chat.

A gulp of courage let her smile at Cameron on the way out. He saluted her with his pen. It was a calm gesture, the gesture of someone who suspected nothing. Or, more likely, had nothing to suspect. And it was cute. He'd sent her an email lamenting that his record was ruined by nine cents, addressed to Katherine. Katie was a common enough nickname, but he didn't have any reason to know her family used it. Was that the only thing that kept him from making the connection? Or was there no connection to make?

Katie mostly put that encounter out of her mind and focused on the hint of her note. Maybe this would be the day a guy who fit the vague description would enter the restaurant. Maybe he'd glance around as though he hoped to find someone who fit the vague description in his mind. Maybe their eyes would meet in a moment of shared searching. It could be so romantic.

And maybe she'd just enjoy her taco salad. She was stabbing around near the bottom of it when Audra came to check on her.

"Is it as good today as it usually is?" she asked.

Katie nodded. "It's wonderful."

Audra flashed a smile at the compliment. Her lips moved a bit. It seemed she wanted to say something else.

"How are you today?" Katie asked by way of invitation.

"Well, not wonderful."

"Why not?"

Audra shook her head in a way that said disgusted was a better way to describe her mood. "You know how sometimes guys send flowers as an apology?"

Katie nodded. She'd never been on the receiving end of a flower apology, but she'd certainly heard of that as a thing.

"Someone got it backwards," Audra said. "I actually got flowers that need an apology."

Katie felt her eyes scrunch up. "What?"

"He sent me flowers at the worst possible time, and he knows it's bad, so that makes it even worse than the worst possible."

"Wow," Katie said. "Is this... can I ask if this guy who sent flowers is the same one you were talking to last week?"

Audra nodded.

"Interesting," Katie said. She wanted to say that at least he was cute, but considering her own situation, she held her tongue. What a guy looked like might only complicate everything. And not knowing was also bad.

"I wonder..." Audra bit her lip, then charged forward with her words. "Have you had any luck solving the mystery you mentioned before?"

The door opened as she spoke. Katie's eyes darted towards the sound. She knew her expression gave away her disappointment when three middle-aged women walked in. "Uh... I think that answers the question."

"So you *are* expecting someone?"

Katie shrugged. She was hoping, not expecting. "Well, if he does ever show up, I might need your help."

"Anything," Audra said.

Katie laughed at the enthusiasm. She didn't tell Audra that the help she might need was access to a back door so she could escape.

There was no need for a back door, yet again. Katie was both relieved and disappointed that Cameron had apparently missed the hint. He wasn't waiting a day or two to be less obvious because she didn't see him – or anyone she thought could be him – for several days. Cameron didn't immediately try another call or press for meeting. Part of her wished he would. She didn't know how much longer she could live with the stress of the unknown. But would knowing help? She wouldn't feel so afraid if knowing could only be good.

She tried to relax and enjoy her lunch breaks. It helped that Audra continued to chat about "inappropriate" gifts. The guy in her life seemed to be trying very hard to overcome whatever timing issue was going on between them. Katie shoved her book aside as Audra approached with a salad. She was eager to hear about any developments.

"So Katie," Audra said. "I'm wondering if, um... Have you ever heard of teach you?"

That wasn't a phrase she'd heard before. It wasn't a flower as far as Katie knew and wondered if it wasn't related to the gifts. She used the location for a possible hint. "No, is that a food?"

Audra gave a short nervous laugh. "That's a good guess because I asked while..." She gestured to the plate she'd set in front of Katie. "I get together with a couple of friends on Friday nights to play a game called Teach You. It's a card game, but it doesn't use a normal deck. You take tricks like Hearts or Spades, but –"

"Wait. How do you spell Teach You?" It suddenly sounded very familiar. Had she been saying it wrong in her head this whole time?

"T-I-C-H-U."

"Oh!" Katie explained that she had heard of it, but didn't realize because she'd only seen it written. She didn't say where she'd seen it written, and Audra didn't ask.

"Well, one of the women I play with, she wants us to replace her because she says we stay up too late. I mean, we're usually done by like 9:30 or so, but she's a little older and... Anyway, would you like to play? Do you know how?"

Katie was momentarily stunned by the invitation. What were the odds she'd find a group of women playing the same game as Cameron on the same night? Friday was common enough for get-togethers, and she never made any effort to keep up with the latest trends. Maybe it wasn't that surprising. Maybe lots of people were playing it. She admitted that she didn't know how.

Audra said she'd be happy to teach and insisted it was a casual, low-key game.

"Great," Katie said. "Yeah. Count me in. You said Fridays, right?" Tomorrow was Friday. Katie wondered how soon she meant.

"Can you come tomorrow?" Audra asked.

Katie grabbed a pen from the top of her bag and got Audra's address and phone number, which she wrote on a napkin. She felt a round of something like gloating at this sudden loophole. Joining a game was not the same as looking up pictures. She was excited to know what Cameron liked. But what if she didn't like it as much? That would be disappointing, but it wouldn't really matter. Katie's dad was a Star Wars fan and her mom was not. They still had a happy marriage.

She hoped she could resist the urge to tell him until after she'd tried the game. It might be better to break it to him gently if she wasn't going to want to join in his favorite pastime in the future. It might have been more difficult if they had a chat going in the evening, but she found a longer letter from him instead.

*Katie,*
*My parents asked me for dinner tonight. You know that's an offer I can't refuse. I'll miss you while I'm with them. I'll probably be thinking of you because I sort of told them. They know I've been trying to find someone online, but I haven't told them much. That's why they're going to ask. A lot. Every time my mom has said anything to me about it, Grandma will be like, "Oh, let's leave him alone." And then she'll look at me like she still expects an answer. My mom is probably talking to her right now saying, "How do you think we can get Cameron to spill his guts about this girl tonight?" It'll be a fun night.*

*I did finish that puzzle last night. And yes, I was kidding about still not knowing what it was. It's a sloth. He's hanging on a tree branch, and that's why there was so much sky. He's not as round as I initially thought. I just had an arm sideways. And yes, you were right to give me a hard time for not thinking that a planet would have space and not sky as a background. I hate to put a puzzle back in the box right after finishing it, but if I leave it out someone might think I don't clean up after myself. I'll give it a few days on the table, then put it away.*

*Why did the chicken cross the road? I don't know, but I didn't hit it. That's not a random joke, it's a random true*

70

*story. There's a house just outside of town that sometimes
has chickens in the front yard. I pass it on my way home from
work. When I came home tonight, one of them was in the
road. It seemed to be coming home from a little jaunt across
the street. I had to slow way down to avoid it. It wasn't a big
deal or even much of an inconvenience. But it got me
thinking about those chickens. I've seen them in the yard a
lot but not in the street before. Have I just been lucky? Are
those chickens in the street all the time and somehow just not
when I drive by? Was that a freak occurrence? How do you
even keep chickens in the yard if you have some? Are those
chickens like pets or are they raised for eggs or food or I don't
know? The whole thing made me think about chickens way
more than I want to. So it was kind of annoying. I know I'll
have to watch carefully on that street from now on because I'll
feel awful if I kill someone's chicken even if it wasn't my fault
it was in the middle of the street.*

*Then I stopped at the grocery store, still thinking about
chicken. I needed a few things, and chicken wasn't one of
them. But I stood in front of packages of raw meat with some
crazy thoughts about trying to cook something. It was crazy
because I knew it wouldn't end well and also because I was
craving chicken after seeing one in the road. I got to say,
chickens don't look remotely appetizing when they're walking
around covered in feathers and feet. Not sure what thought
process got me wanting to eat some. I ended up getting a bag
of frozen breaded chicken pieces. It's precooked so I only
have to warm it up. I can do that. Since someone's cooking
for me tonight, it'll probably be tomorrow.*

*There was a minor mystery waiting for me when I got home.
A green colored pencil was on the table. By itself. Just one
random colored pencil sitting in the middle of the table. As
far as I know, neither of us owns any colored pencils. I don't
think I've used any since school, and I don't remember
packing any when I moved out. I've never seen Elijah doing
any coloring or drawing. And if he was, how could he have
left just one sitting in such an obvious place? If it was on the
floor, I might have guessed he was working on something and*

didn't realize he dropped one. It's weird. If he gets up before I turn in, I'll have to ask him about it.

I heard on the radio a kind of stupid contest where people were calling in to guess the date of the first frost this year. It was stupid because they were calling it a contest, but it wasn't really. They weren't recording guesses or offering a prize. They were just encouraging people to call in to argue about it. I mean, it was a good-natured argument. People were inventing ridiculous reasons to support their guesses. One woman said she had looked up the dates of the first frosts for the last twenty years and calculated an average for her guess and another simply said she always thought eleven was a lucky number. There was a guy who said you could tell when the frost would hit by tasting the grass. I honestly don't know if he was being serious or not because he sounded serious but... well, he said you should have started tasting the grass by the first of September so you'd recognize when it turned bitter, which would be no more than twenty-four hours before the first frost. I actually sat in the parking lot of the grocery store for a few minutes to listen to him finish explaining that you don't have to eat the grass, you just bite it and spit it out. That's why it bugged me. I knew it was ridiculous, and yet I was totally sucked in. And I'm just realizing as I write that grass guy never even gave a guess. It felt wrong to listen to talk about frost when it was over eighty today. But I suppose the unseasonably warm weather was what got people talking about cooler days ahead. I thought it was nice today, by the way.

And now I'm talking about the weather. Is it obvious that I'm trying to think of things to write? That's because the only thing I can think is how much I want to meet you. I've been trying not to write that because I know you're reluctant to take that step. I need to be honest though. I think it's past time to meet. I think we're afraid of the same thing. And maybe afraid to admit it. It's clear that we get along well, at least in print. I think the biggest obstacle to translate this to real life would be if one or both of us feels no physical attraction. But that is part of a relationship, and the longer we wait to find *out, the harder it will be for someone, probably you, to give the just friends speech.*

*If I'm wrong and there's something else that scares you, tell me. If I'm not wrong, let's go for it. You can set all the terms, the time and place and how to be recognized and whatever. How busy is your weekend?*
  *Cameron*

9

It was fortunate that Katie wasn't normally a fidgety person. Her office mates were looking at her with more curiosity than irritation when she realized she was loudly tapping her pen against her desk, and that she hadn't just started.

"Sorry," she said.

"Ready for the weekend, Katherine?"

She continued to smile apologetically but didn't comment. She was not ready for the weekend. There was one thing she needed to do, one thing she had convinced herself was necessary. But now she wasn't so sure. Why did love have to be so confusing?

Using Courting Catholics was supposed to make it simpler. Katie expected that the hard part would be finding a compatible guy. Once they had established that they shared important values and dreamed of a similar future, she thought she'd be excited to meet him. As long as he had an attractive personality, it wouldn't really matter how he looked. That would change as they grew old together.

And how often in her day-to-day life did Katie encounter a man who was repulsive? Hardly ever. It was almost always something in his manners or activities that made her want to move away. She'd never been the type of girl anyone would describe as boy crazy. She read Christian romance novels, but she liked to see how the characters got along and how they found each other. She rolled her eyes at the swoony parts.

Cameron's last letter made her face a truth she'd been trying to deny. She wanted swoony. Or rather, she didn't want to give it up. Katie had started a response to his letter as soon as she finished reading it. She intended to explain that a lack of physical attraction was not what worried her because she was sure it would grow from a solid relationship even if it wasn't there immediately. Then she would tease him for listening to a guy talk about chewing on grass and tell him a sloth should have been easy to recognize.

Her message had faltered in the first sentence though. She wrote that she only wanted more time to establish that solid foundation. She thought she believed that, but it felt wrong somehow. She changed her wording several times, trying to convey that the physical component of a marriage was the least important and that it would fade anyway. Any initial attraction would need to be replaced with a desire to maintain the relationship no matter what. There had to be loving actions even when there were no loving feelings. Only then would they want to stay close even when one of them had red eyes and a runny nose or forty pounds of pregnancy weight.

The words were true, but regardless of how Katie arranged them the sentiment felt less than honest. She deleted her message and prepared to start over. It occurred to her that she couldn't speak for both of them. Maybe she was more afraid that Cameron wouldn't find *her* attractive.

That idea hit a nerve. Hard. Katie began to type out that confession. As she did so, she reasoned that he was absolutely right. If that was her fear, then waiting longer to find out would only hurt more than knowing now. And yet she still couldn't bring herself to agree to meet. She was admitting an embarrassing insecurity and admitting that moving forward was a more logical choice than letting it fester. But something still held her back.

Katie abandoned any attempt to write a message and sat on her comfortable sofa with her Bible. She opened it to St. Paul's words on love, reflecting on the question. Love rejoices in the truth and is not pompous. She read the chapter three times, then closed her eyes in a bid to see the truth. Why was she standing in her own way?

The truth was ugly. Katie didn't want to meet Cameron because she didn't want to stop thinking of him as the guy at work who made her breath catch. She didn't want to stop walking by the other Cameron's desk while she pictured him writing notes to the fabulous and mysterious woman behind the keyboard. She was caught up in a romantic daydream and using a real-life guy to perpetuate it. That was so wrong. No wonder she didn't want to face it.

She sent no messages while she processed the situation. Before she went to bed, she convinced herself that it was necessary to sever the daydream first. The plan was to march into that other office and see Cameron objectively as a coworker who happened to be nice-looking but with no hopes or fantasy attached. Once she proved to herself she could do that, Katie could contact Cameron – the real Cameron – about when they could meet and find out if they had any hope of a future together.

Katie flattened her hand against her desk to silence the pen she was tapping again. She sent a surreptitious glance around the room. No one was glaring at her. Yet. She sort of felt like glaring at herself. The note for Connie was still sitting where she'd written it nearly an hour ago. She kept coming up with tasks to accomplish ahead of that one. It was nearly lunchtime. This had to be done. It was important to her plan whether it was a good one or not. She picked up her sticky note and moved away from the safety of her desk.

Months. It had to have been months since that light started flickering. How had no one fixed it yet? How was it not completely dead? A dim spot would be an improvement. Katie felt a mild satisfaction at focusing on the mundane complaint. This was just an office, not a factory for romantic notions. She smiled as she passed the open door of her boss's office. He nodded stiffly. She even turned towards the doorway she usually ignored, gave a casual smile to no one in particular. She trained her eyes on the floor as she entered the larger room around the corner, then aimed her eyes at Connie. She was prepared to notice Cameron only out of her peripheral vision. Her experiment of seeing him as nothing more than the guy who did a nice job checking his work failed. It failed because she didn't see him at all.

"Hi, Connie," she said.

"Katherine." Connie said the name as though she was simply stating the fact that she was in front of her. There was no invitation to communicate.

Katie plastered the sticky note to her desk. "I got another call about this one," she said. "Management's probably going to get involved soon. Have you had a chance to look into it?"

Connie sighed and closed her eyes against the annoyance of the question. "I have so much work to do. Just leave it there."

"Okay. Have a nice day." Katie turned away wondering if her cheery tone sounded patronizing. That wasn't her intent. It took a huge amount of effort to not let Connie make her feel as though she was a pest for doing her job. Maybe she was overcompensating.

"Hey, Katherine. Ready for the weekend?" It was a common Friday question addressed to her with sympathetic eyes, eyes that said he didn't think she was a pest. That helped.

She paused for a moment next to Cameron's empty chair. Where was he? "I guess. This place isn't so bad though, is it, Mike?"

He shook his head. His eyes bounced to Connie and back. "No," he said. "Home is just better."

"I have to agree with that, and I hope you enjoy your weekend." She and Mike shared a friendly smile as she resumed her walk to the hallway.

The hallway was empty except for her questions about Cameron. Was he out sick today? Or had he only stepped away from his desk for the two minutes Katie was in the room? Why did it matter? Why did it matter to Katie that he wasn't there? Because if she could convince herself that she was only curious and not disappointed to miss a chance to indulge her mushy feelings, then maybe it was proof enough she was ready to let go of that fantasy.

Katie turned around under the flickering light. She hadn't convinced herself of anything, and pacing seemed better than disturbing her office mates. What if Cameron was here somewhere, and she bumped into him in the hallway? Katie could picture saying hello as he approached, possibly asking if he was ready for the weekend. That would be a nonchalant exchange no different than with any other coworker. But no matter how clearly she imagined it, she knew she had a good imagination. It wasn't real without his physical presence. Her response to that was what she needed to regulate.

Two people passed her at different times. If either of them passed her again, her lingering in the hallway would raise questions. Katie wasn't about to answer that she was hoping to run into a particular person without feeling all fluttery. She returned to her desk. She stayed only long enough to make sure it was orderly, grab her purse, and let a few people know she was headed out to lunch.

The January Café had a wide chrome frame on the door that gave the place a retro vibe. Katie didn't know what time period that was popular or even if it was associated with a certain era. There was just something about it that made her think "classic," and that something may not have been prompted by anything beyond her opinion. She shook her head, concluding that it could be added to the list of features she liked about the restaurant without confusing herself with why.

She sat in her usual corner spot, smiling at Audra on her way. She opened her book instead of her menu since she already knew what she would order. The door opened as soon as she got comfortable and a woman with two small children entered. The smaller one was perched on her hip and the older one, who might have been five or so, held her hand. Katie pondered for a moment how the woman had opened the door with both of her hands full. Then her mind turned to whether or not she'd ever have a chance to feel so competent in the role of mom. Mooning over an uninterested and possibly incompatible coworker would not get her closer to that goal.

"Hi, Katie."

Smiling up at Audra, Katie said, "Hi! How are you today?"

"Pretty good," Audra said. Her smile and the light in her eyes made that sound like an understatement. Audra usually looked fairly sunny, but something about her seemed to glow more than normal. "Taco salad?"

"Absolutely. Do you want me to try to find the rules of Tichu so I can read up on it before tonight?"

"Hmm." Audra suddenly appeared more serious and tipped her head to consider the question.

Katie thought of Cameron informing her that Tichu was very important and smiled to think he might have given similar deliberation.

"No," Audra said after a moment. "I mean, you can if you want, but I think I'll feel the need to start at the beginning when I explain it so I don't leave anything out. You might get annoyed if I'm going over basics you've already read."

"Okay. I'll wait for your instructions."

"If only everyone was so wise," Audra said jokingly. "Back in a minute with your lunch."

The salad was as delicious as always. Audra was busy with the lunch crowd. She still found time to walk by with an occasional comment like, "Someone just ordered mac and cheese and asked for a ton of garlic sprinkled on top. Glad he's leaving when he's done." Or "I'm on my way to the kitchen to read the ingredients on the ketchup bottle."

Katie continued to watch the door but with more peace than

she had been. She was still nervous about the possibility of seeing someone who could be Cameron. She no longer hoped to stay hidden though. If he seemed to notice her, she could say in a message that they might have seen each other. Then he would have a better idea if he really wanted to meet.

There were no likely candidates before she finished her lunch. Audra returned to take payment and lingered at the table after she returned the card. "You are excited about tonight, right?"

Katie nodded. "I am. I just hope your friends are as welcoming to a newbie."

"They will be."

"What were you talking about earlier when you said you were reading the ketchup bottle?"

Audra rolled her eyes. She checked over her shoulder and lowered her voice. "There's a group of guys – other side of the restaurant – and one of them wanted me to make sure tomatoes are the first ingredient listed on our ketchup."

"Why?"

"I didn't ask," Audra said. "But when I told him it was, he wanted a whole dish next to his burger as well as some on it. I think maybe he's hoping if he eats enough it'll count as a vegetable."

Katie laughed as she picked up her purse.

"Remind me tonight to tell you what happened in the kitchen."

"Okay. I'll see you then." Katie waved and made her way to the door. She glanced back at the other side and spotted the guy dipping a burger in a bowl of ketchup. At least that was better than garlic-crusted macaroni. But then she realized the guy next to him seemed rather young. He had brown hair. Could he be twenty-four? Probably not. He looked older. Katie was debating about an excuse to head back inside – a quick trip to the restroom maybe – when he reached for something and she saw a wedding ring. Not Cameron. She was more disappointed than relieved for a change.

The afternoon was better, sort of. Fridays generally had Katie's lightest workload. The time passed faster when she was busy though. She had a nice chat with a couple of coworkers who did most of the talking, and she didn't really think about trying to visit Cameron's office.

She did think about it. The idea from the morning was still in the back of her mind. She was sad that she missed him. Not trying again felt like the better option. She didn't need to prove anything. She only needed to focus on the real Cameron. He held her hopes.

After a quick dinner at home, Katie had about an hour before she needed to leave for Audra's game. She opened her laptop. There were no new messages from Cameron. He was likely waiting to hear how his push to meet had been received. Katie sorted through her thoughts before she began to put them into words. She wanted to tell him she was ready to meet, though still terrified. She needed to confess that she'd been hoping to get a glimpse of him at the restaurant he mentioned. Did he even remember letting that slip? She hesitated at addressing his suggestion of that very weekend. It felt so soon and sudden. And yet the idea of waiting another week in suspense now that she was ready to meet wasn't much more appealing. Should they send pictures? Katie still didn't have a good one. She hadn't even given it another attempt. Surely she'd make a better impression in person than in one of those awkward poses.

The phone asked for her attention. Katie thought about ignoring it, but it was the family ring. She peeked at the screen. Cecelia. That wasn't surprising since the others mostly texted. And Cecelia was now less than a week from her due date. The possibility of news was enough incentive to answer.

"I did it!" Cecelia exclaimed.

"Did what?" Katie asked, though she doubted that "had a baby" was the answer.

"I finished work."

"Uh, yeah."

"Why don't you sound happier for me?"

"I am happy for you," Katie said. "I'm just not surprised. You've had this planned as your last day for a month."

"Well, if the baby had come early, I might have left some loose ends."

"Maybe." Katie closed the laptop to concentrate on her sister. "But if you were holding a baby right now, I doubt you'd care."

Cecelia spoke with a wistful tone. "You're right. I am so ready to hold a baby. I know it'll be an even bigger change than I think, but I can't wait to be able to sit down without pushing a foot out of my ribs."

Katie smiled to herself. The last time she saw Cecelia, she had looked kind of uncomfortable.

"Thank you for not trying to correct me," Cecelia said. "If I had said something like that to Liz, she would have assured me I had no idea how big the change will be. She can be kind of smug about her experience."

Liz hadn't seemed smug to Katie at all. She thought Cecelia had probably been oversensitive about something. But suggesting an oversensitive person might be oversensitive was like lighting a match in a fireworks factory. Katie tried to be diplomatic. "I guess I'll be lucky both of you will be experienced if I ever have a turn."

"Oh, yes. I will give you lots of good advice even before you know to ask for it." Cecelia sounded as though she was trying not to laugh. It seemed she was humble enough to know she would one day be just as smug.

"I look forward to that," Katie said, only half joking.

Cecelia gasped at a sudden idea. "You haven't told anyone the name, have you?"

"Of course not," Katie said. "I can keep a secret."

"I know. But I also know it's hard. I have almost said it myself a few times, especially around Mom."

"She'll be happy," Katie said. Cecelia planned to make their mom's first name the baby's middle name. When she was stitching it onto the Christmas ornament, they both smiled at how pleased their mom would be to see it hanging on her tree. Katie was going to comment that she wasn't having trouble waiting, not to point out differences between her and Cecelia but to assure her the secret would be kept. Thinking of waiting, however, caused her to glance at the clock. "Oh, I have to go."

"What!?" Cecelia cried. "You have something more important to do than talk to your sister?"

She was kidding, but her penchant for drama made it slightly uncomfortable to play along. Katie said, "Yes, I do."

"Oh, wait. Is it a date?"

"No. I'm just meeting some new friends."

"If you're finally meeting some guys you've been talking to online," Cecelia said, "you should meet them one at a time."

Katie ignored the sarcastic advice. "This has nothing to do with that."

"But *have* you met anyone?" Cecelia pressed.

"Not yet. And I really do need to go or I'll be late."

"Oh, *yet* sounds promising. I'll call you tomorrow to get details."

Katie put the phone down smiling at her sister's insistence that there was something to share. Cecelia would definitely keep her word to call again and try very hard to get details. Katie could keep a secret though. She might tell her she was working on a possibility just to tease her. She wouldn't reveal Cameron's name until a few meetings went well, if they went well. It was time to leave for Audra's. Even the unfinished letter to Cameron was going to have to wait for details.

10

That unfinished letter stayed in the back of Katie's mind during the drive. She was forming her suggestion for how and when they should meet. Sunday afternoon sounded good to her. She was generally peaceful after church. They could have a casual lunch at Burger Brothers. The restaurant in town was owned by a couple of guys – brothers, obviously – and Katie thought one of them was a little scary. That's why she rarely ate there. If the date went poorly, she wouldn't have to worry about bad memories ruining a place she liked. And if it went well, maybe she'd have someone to go with her to talk to the scary guy. The burgers were delicious.

A burger was a sandwich that required cooking. Katie was surprised she hadn't thought of that before. It was a great reason to convince Cameron the meeting place would work. The sticking point of the plan was how to recognize him. She still really wanted to spot him first. If there were no other thirtyish women in the place, she would be recognizable right away, too. She was willing to take that risk as long as she knew she was looking at the right guy. And maybe she could plan to be there early, hiding behind a book or something. Yes, she was scheming for a brief but unfair advantage, but if Cameron didn't want to give it to her, he shouldn't have said she could name all the terms.

Katie turned onto Audra's street and shoved aside her scheming. The address looked more like a large house than an apartment building, but the line of mailboxes out front suggested there were several occupants. She parked her car and scanned the street. She was enjoying the song on the radio, but that was only part of the reason she didn't immediately shut off the car. She tapped the beat on the steering wheel as she took in all the cars on the street. Audra could be here already. They were supposed to meet when Audra got home from work. A pickup truck parked nearby only seconds after Katie had stopped. The woman who got out had a long, brown ponytail. Audra was blonde. She walked up to the big house so she must be the other card player. She looked about as young as Audra. Katie hoped she didn't feel like the old person among them.

The woman who answered the door wasn't Audra either. Katie began to feel silly hiding in her car. Surely Audra had told her roommate to expect someone new. She shut off the music and the engine, then reached for her purse. As she opened her door, another car parked. Katie got out and saw that the woman driving the other car was Audra. She walked down the sidewalk to meet her.

Audra waved and stopped near her car. "You haven't been waiting long, have you?"

"No. Just a minute," Katie said. "I think your other friend just got here, too."

Audra's eyes moved to the truck, and she nodded. "Great. We'll be able to start right away."

Katie gestured towards the huge house they were approaching. "I almost drove right past. Since your address included a letter, I was expecting something more, uh… less mansiony." She'd expected a square building with symmetrical lettered doors and not the turreted house with a brick sidewalk circling it.

"Yeah, it's a cool house even if I only get one corner of it. It used to be all one house, but… well, that was long enough ago that I never got to see it." Audra led her to the left door and stuck her key

85

in the lock. Two other women jumped up from the couch as they entered.

Katie tried to look friendly as she waited for Audra to make introductions.

"Okay, everyone, this is Katie." Audra pointed to the woman with dark, curly hair pinned high on her head. "That's Violet. She's the one who lives with me. And that's Alison. She's dating my brother."

The women nodded and said hello. Audra told Katie she was welcome to set her purse on the counter before she ducked through a doorway that appeared to lead to her bedroom.

"We know you're a January Café fan," Violet said.

Katie nodded. "Definitely," she said. "I think I'd be eating there all the time even if…" She bit her lip to keep from finishing that sentence. Audra knew she had a reason other than lunch for frequenting the place, but she didn't know what that reason was or how embarrassing it was. Katie thought leading with foolishness would not be her best impression.

Audra returned from her room to distract everyone from the incomplete thought. "Where do you work?" she asked. "It must be close to make us a convenient lunch stop."

"Yeah." Katie blew out a quick breath at the neutral topic. "It's a place called EJ Industries. I do accounts payable."

"I've heard of that," Audra said. She tapped her temple as though trying to jog loose a memory.

"It's on 105, about halfway between here and Andauk."

Audra continued to squint thoughtfully.

"Accounts payable?" Alison said. "You write checks all day?"

"Something like that."

"Do you like it?" Violet asked. She appeared genuinely interested.

Katie shrugged. She liked parts of her job. Not the parts that required her to chase down coworkers and point out their mistakes.

She explained that while they all moved closer to the table.

She got three sympathetic looks in response to her description. Audra gestured to the chair across from her at the same time so Katie took that one. They would be a team against Violet and Alison. Audra took the cards out of the box and fanned them out on the table as she began to communicate the rules of Tichu. Katie smiled to herself as she pictured relaying some of this to Cameron later. She could surprise him with her new knowledge on the date. That would give them something to talk about.

The cards looked different than Katie expected. Cameron said they were like regular cards but with different suits. These cards did run two through ace with four different colored suits. But they were still somehow not what she'd expected. Busier perhaps? There were also four special cards. Audra told her that playing the one with a picture of a dog gave your partner the lead. Then she held it up and said, "There are times it's okay to give your partner the dog, but for now just don't, okay?"

Katie said, "Okay," even though she didn't understand. By the knowing smiles around her, it was clear that Audra did not like to have the dog, and that was the important point. Katie paid close attention to learn how and when it would be relevant. Audra went over the basics and dealt out a practice hand. The women played that round with all the cards showing so Katie could learn from each of them. It was starting to make sense, though she could see the nuances would take practice.

As Violet began to deal out the real game, Katie told Audra that she'd asked to be reminded about something that happened in the kitchen earlier.

"Oh, right," Audra said, smiling at a memory. "There's this kid named Ben who does some cooking. I mean, he's eighteen so he's not that much... It's weird that he seems like a kid to me. Anyway, he jumped in front of me as I went into the kitchen during lunch this afternoon, and he said, 'I lost the cranberries,' with this panicked expression. It was all I could do to keep from laughing because it was very sudden and confusing. He motioned me over to the stove where he was working on a dish. He had a bag of dried cranberries nearby that had apparently disappeared, and he was afraid Ryan was going to be mad."

"Did you find them?" Alison asked.

"Ryan would help him find them," Violet said at the same time.

Audra nodded at both of them. "We were still trying to figure out what happened when Ryan showed up and pointed out that the bag had slipped down a crack between the stove and the table next to it. I give him a hard time about yelling at the employees, but he's actually pretty patient. It was funny to me that Ben is apparently a bit scared of him. The look on his face when he said, 'I lost the cranberries,' was kind of priceless."

Alison chuckled with the others at Audra's imitation of panic but was the first to sober. "Trevor has said your grandparents are impressed with the job Ryan's doing."

"Trevor?" Katie's ears perked up.

"That's my other brother," Audra said. "The one who thinks Alison is amazing."

Katie stared hard at the cards she was sorting to appear that they were the cause of her concentration. She was fixated on the names though. She knew Audra's oldest brother was named Ryan. Audra had pointed him out as the manager at the January Café. Ryan was a fairly common name so it had meant nothing to her. But Trevor? She had brothers named Ryan *and* Trevor? That couldn't be a coincidence. What were the odds of two brothers with the same names in the same town? It didn't matter. They had to be the same guys who played Tichu with Cameron. That was something else she could talk to him about. It was true that she'd been hanging out at one of his favorite places, but Katie still felt God's hand in all of this. No one else could have orchestrated her meeting the people around Cameron like this.

The game progressed somewhat slowly. Katie still had fun. She was happy to understand why Cameron liked it so much. Maybe someday she'd be able to play with him. She sensed a competitive streak though. She'd need to improve before she could be his partner. Audra patiently corrected Katie's beginner mistakes and didn't appear to blame her when they lost. She said it was because luck wasn't on their side and smiled as she put the cards away.

"Now for part two of the evening," Audra said. "We go bother the guys."

The other two women immediately stood up with Audra.

"Bother the guys?" Katie asked. No one had told her anything about a part two of the evening. And the only guys who had been mentioned were Audra's brothers, who – unless there were some astronomically weird coincidences going on – would be with Cameron right now.

"I told you my brothers live next door, right?"

Katie sort of nodded as she rose from her chair. Audra had said her brother also lived next door when she pointed out that they worked together. Alison had mentioned Trevor a few other times but never in the context of him being next door.

"They have their own Tichu game, and we like to end by seeing how they're doing," Audra explained. "Alison likes the excuse to say hello to Trevor, and Violet... uh, Violet and I like to say hello, too. And tonight, I'm excited to introduce you, too. Though you sort of met Ryan at the restaurant."

"Yeah, I..." Four guys with a regular Tichu night? Coincidences had been thoroughly ruled out. "Well, I've seen him anyway."

"Great, let's go." Audra shooed everyone out ahead of her.

Violet and Alison knew where they were going. Katie followed them having a little trouble breathing. This was so perfect. She was going to get an anonymous glimpse of Cameron after all. She could tell him in her letter that he now knew what she looked like. He could decide if he thought there could be a spark without having to be face to face to do it. The other ladies stopped just short of a side door to let Audra be the one to knock.

She didn't though. She rang the bell repeatedly, then let herself in without waiting for an answer.

Alison smiled at what was, to her, expected before she followed Violet. Katie went in last. The friendly greetings she walked into suggested no one was bothered by the intrusion. At the end of a brief hall, four guys were sitting around a card table. Katie only really saw one of them. Recognition threatened her composure. She forced herself to speak and at least prove she wasn't speechless.

"Oh! Hi, Cameron." Her voice came out higher than normal.

Cameron West looked up from the cards and did a double take. "Katherine? Hi."

The greeting was neutral. Mostly. His tone had mild surprise but nothing that indicated he suspected anything other than the minor fluke of running into a coworker outside of work.

Audra had raised eyebrows though. She had noticed the use of Katie's full name. *Please don't make a big deal out of it,* Katie thought. She didn't want to explain away the only cover she had at the moment. She needed to get home and wrap her head around what to do next before anyone asked any questions.

Fortunately, Audra asked Cameron how they knew each other. And she called her Katherine, too.

"From work," he said.

"Oh, that's why it sounded familiar when you told me..." Something to the side caught Audra's eye and caused her to gasp. "What have you guys done?" She pulled something out of her pocket as she rushed to a painting on the wall. Was that a level? Audra carried a level in her pocket? Katie was grateful that her friend was a little weird because it drew all the attention in the room. She was grateful until she chanced a glance at Cameron and saw he was amused by it.

Audra was closer to his age. She had that beautiful blonde hair nearly to her elbows and a cute nose with no glasses perched on it.

"What did you think of the game?" Ryan asked. "Will you be back next week?"

It took Katie a moment to realize he was talking to her. A moment was long enough for Audra to answer instead.

"Of course she will," she said.

"Tichu is awesome," one of the other guys said. Based on the family resemblance and the fact that Alison had a hand on his shoulder, he must be the other brother, Trevor. "How could she not like it?"

"I guess there's only one way to answer that," Katie said, glad she enjoyed the game enough to laugh at the pressure to say so. She was also glad the pressure could be an excuse for her blush. Her face felt about a thousand degrees. Her incredible awareness of Cameron paired with her efforts not to look at him also made her increasingly uncomfortable.

"I bet Violet was a good teacher," Ryan said.

Katie began to nod.

"*I* taught her," Audra interrupted. "And who do you think taught Violet?"

It was a good thing Audra kept hiding her pauses. Katie was having trouble following the conversation. Blood pounded in her ears as though she'd been running hard. The others were talking without her. Something about the score and whose turn it was. What was happening? All that time Katie had spent trying to discover whether the two Camerons were the same guy, she knew now that she'd never really believed it possible. She might have even convinced herself she'd imagined that flash of a familiar logo on his screen. The shock was too great. She hadn't thought this could actually happen.

Katie needed a lifeline, something unemotional for her thoughts to grab. Her eyes roved the room, carefully avoiding

Cameron, and landed on a row of Tichu suits painted on the edge of the table. Her fingers brushed over the smooth surface. Did anyone else notice them trembling? "Wow. You have a custom table?"

Trevor nodded and pointed proudly over his shoulder. "Alison made it."

"I didn't *make* it," she said. "I just refinished it."

"It's great," Katie said. What a bland compliment. She needed to get out of this room.

Trevor and Alison thanked her simultaneously.

The guys were still placing cards on the table. Cameron played calmly, at least as far as she could decern from her traitorous eyes constantly darting his direction. She was trying to control them. Audra announced two of the guys winners. Katie didn't follow which two. She didn't even know the game was about to end. Did that mean she could leave?

"Plenty of time," Cameron said.

*Time for what? Please no one talk to me*, Katie thought. *I don't know what's going on.*

"Good idea," the still unnamed guy said. Wait. Logan. That was what Audra had said was the name of the guy sending her inappropriate flowers. How had that one coherent thought made it through the jumble in her head?

He stood and said, "Let me just walk the ladies out first."

Katie moved towards the door. Violet was near her, but she didn't open it. The others were talking and laughing. Was it time to leave or not? Everyone but Cameron was standing up now. Were they all leaving? Violet moved back into the room. But Alison took her place and motioned Katie to head through the open door first. The fresh air and absence of stifling hormones cleared her head. Katie forced herself to turn back to Audra as they exited. "This was fun," she said. It was fun until her brain fell apart. "We're definitely on for the same time next week?"

Audra nodded eagerly. "And we'll talk before then about, um…" She gestured to the door behind her.

Katie knew she meant the weird vibes she'd sensed while they were inside. "I think we have to," she said. She would have to confess enough for Audra to know to keep it secret. She pushed Cameron to the back of her head for one more minute of politeness. "Nice to meet you, Logan."

He smiled but already had his eyes on Audra. Katie kept her head clear long enough to exchange a few pleasant words with Alison before they split to their respective vehicles. Katie pulled away from the curb trying to process what she now knew. Was there the slightest chance the enthusiasm in Cameron's messages could be transferred to the boring old woman he barely saw at work?

11

After a night of tossing and turning, Katie woke up feeling that she needed to talk to Audra. That wasn't the predominant feeling. She was tired and frazzled and wondering if talking to Audra would even help. But Audra knew Cameron, at least a little. It seemed she was the only person who might be able to offer advice.

Had Katie missed something in one of their exchanges? She thought she'd been looking for hints, but now she wasn't so sure. The shock of the previous night told her that her mind had been closed to the possibility of the two Camerons being one and the same. There was no way she'd have been so shocked if she really believed it was possible. She spent several hours – not on purpose, the time kept getting away from her – rereading Cameron's words to her. She freely imaged the guy from work behind them now. Not with a fanciful hope but a face-flaming dread. If he knew who she was...

The embarrassing introspection was interrupted by a call from Cecelia. Katie was more adamant than ever about keeping her love life private so they mostly chatted about Cecelia's swollen body and the cute outfit she planned for her baby's first posed pictures.

It was nearly dinnertime before Audra returned her call. They began with the usual small talk, but Audra didn't waste much time in rooting out the reason for the call. "Your message sounded like you had something specific to talk about," she said.

"Yeah, I... How long have you known Cameron?"

"He's been playing Tichu with my brothers a little over a year."
The statement was matter-of-fact, but Audra's tone was all raised
eyebrows and question.

Katie dove into her story. She jumped over the crush to start
where she'd been messaging a guy with the same name as someone
at work without any real thoughts it could be the same guy. She
explained how he'd mentioned the January Café, and that was when
she'd started having lunch there to try to spot someone who matched
his description.

At this revelation, an odd muted squeal came through the
phone.

"Are you okay?" Katie asked.

"Yes. Mostly." Audra sounded a little out of breath. "I just
can't believe you've been looking for someone I know this whole
time. And you figured it out last night?"

"Yeah."

"How? I mean, you've seen Cameron before. How did you
know he was the guy online?"

Katie relayed how the names and the Tichu game let her know
she was about to come face-to-face with her modern pen pal and
how shocked she'd been to recognize him.

"You seemed a little... off," Audra said. "I thought you were
just nervous about new people and I was imagining that it was a big
deal."

"Oh, great. I bet Cameron thinks I'm a nutcase now."

"I doubt he noticed anything." Audra made a scoffing noise.
"I mentioned to Logan about how Cameron called you Katherine
instead of Katie, and he was like so what. Guys aren't nearly as
perceptive as we are."

"Hmm." Katie hoped Audra knew what she was talking about.

"So how can I help?" Audra asked. "I love playing
matchmaker."

"Um…" Katie wasn't sure that matchmaker was the job title she was looking for.

"Have you told him? I mean, how did he react?"

"I haven't, um…"

"Figured out what to say?" Audra finished. "I understand. You want to get the wording just right."

"I don't think I want to tell him." Katie realized how true that was as the words left her mouth. She had thought she was looking for encouragement, but Audra's enthusiasm was meeting a ton of resistance.

"What!? Why not?"

"I know he'll be disappointed," Katie said. "He's never shown any interest in me at work, and then when he knows it'll be so awkward when I run into him."

"He's not going to be disappointed. You said he was excited to meet you."

"To *meet* me. When he finds out he already knows me…" Katie didn't want to detail the letdown.

"When you say he hasn't shown any interest, what does that mean? Just because he hasn't asked you out in person?"

"No. I mean, he hasn't. We just… haven't talked much."

Audra sucked in a breath so fast it was almost a gasp. Or maybe she gasped. "Did *you* have, or do you have any interest? You must have been paying attention to him to know if he was paying attention to you. Now that you know what he looks like, you still want to meet, right?"

Katie heard the air quotes around the word meet. She mostly heard that Audra wanted to know exactly how cute she thought Cameron was. Her face was heating up with no one else in the room. Admitting a one-sided attraction was not easy, particularly to someone who might use the information to try to do some matchmaking. Katie wanted to casually mention that his appearance wasn't a problem for her and quickly move on to more pressing matters, but she was mentally stumbling over what was pressing. Why had she called Audra if not for a pep talk before talking to Cameron? Why had she even gotten Audra involved?

Because Audra was already peripherally involved and didn't know it. It was important to fill her in so she didn't inadvertently let something slip in front of Cameron. "It's not going to work out," Katie said flatly. "And I might need you to cover for me."

"How?"

"Well, if there's going to be repeats of what you call part two of Friday nights... I think, at least for a while, I'm going to have trouble acting naturally. It'll be hard not to reveal things I shouldn't know. Since you'll know why, you could maybe distract people if I get tongue-tied, try to call me Katherine, maybe even change the subject if we're headed in the wrong direction."

"Hmm," Audra said. "I would much rather help you two get together than help keep you apart."

Katie laughed at the disappointed attitude. It mirrored her own, except perhaps the interfering part, but it was past time to give up on the fantasy. Audra continued to try to convince her to tell Cameron. Though nothing she said caused concern that she might go against Katie's wishes and tell him herself. Katie ended the call feeling that she had an ally. It was right to confide in someone, someone who could offer emotional support if this was more difficult than expected.

Katie read the last message she had been composing to Cameron. Only one day ago, she had sounded hopeful that a meeting would go well. She deleted her unfinished thoughts. There was nothing new from Cameron. He was still silent, still waiting. Katie began a new message. She thought this for the best, truly believed she was saving him from having to hide his disappointment if he found out who she was. But she knew that he wouldn't know that. He wouldn't know why, and she hated how sudden and confusing it would feel to him.

*Cameron,*

*As much as I have enjoyed getting to know you these last few months, I have come to the conclusion that our relationship would not survive the shift to in person. If we can't meet face-to-face, and I believe we can't, then it is probably in everyone's best interest if we stop communicating altogether. I'm sorry.*

*Katie*

\*\*\*\*

The final note had been impersonal and detached. A clean break, though not exactly a breakup. The friendship they'd formed in writing had been real because Katie felt the loss. There was an empty place where she'd gotten in the habit of compiling mental notes on her day. She talked to Liz Sunday night, who reminded her of one of Noah's old pranks. Katie didn't need to pick out the best details when she knew there was no one to whom she would relay the story later. She drove to work Monday thinking of chickens on the road. It wasn't funny when she knew she couldn't playfully blame Cameron for the image later.

Naturally, she found an issue with one of Connie's files by the end of the morning. Katie knew it would only be a matter of time before she bumped into Cameron at work. She had hoped to have more time. She considered sending the question in an email. That would be about as effective. But it would be cowardly. And it would be unprofessional to let something outside of work affect how she conducted herself at work. She thought about waiting until Cameron would likely be at lunch and just leaving a sticky note on Connie's desk. That had the same arguments against it, in addition to making Katie hungry with a late lunch for herself.

She was going to choose bravery. She grabbed her note and marched into the hallway, where her steps immediately slowed. Her courage wasn't failing. She was distracted by the fact that something was different. The light had been fixed. She'd gotten so used to the flickering that she barely noticed it anymore. Of all the things that had gone wrong lately, she had to shake her head that it was something so insignificant that was fixed. She shrugged off the change and continued her mission.

This was one of those simple but not easy things. All she had to do was walk in and out of his office without looking at Cameron in a way that told him she knew everything he'd written to her. Katie was positive her eyes were not that expressive. But the rest of her body was bound to give away that something wasn't right. Her legs were wobbly and her arms were swinging unnaturally. She pulled herself together with a hyper-focused beeline for Connie's desk.

"Good morning, Connie," she said.

Connie said nothing but gave Katie a moment of impatient attention.

"Can you look at this file when you get a minute? I don't understand why Old Kingdom is billing us only about a quarter of what you billed the customer."

"Shouldn't receivables be concerned about how much I billed the customer?" Connie managed to roll her eyes during the entire length of her question.

"Yes," Katie said. She had no doubt that someone from accounts receivable would ask Connie about the same number. "But your expected payout is higher, too, and I need to know if I should be looking for a corrected invoice from Old Kingdom or if you've included another file. Which one is it?"

"Why does it matter? Just pick another file if there's extra money."

Katie took a few slow, even breaths. She was going to lose her patience if she stood there and tried to explain her job to Connie. Again. "I can't pick another file at random because if it's the wrong one, then nothing will match up with the right one. And the invoice for the wrong one will eventually show up to cause more problems."

Connie shook her head as though Katie was the one who didn't understand. "What exactly do you want from me?"

"Look up this file. Write down which shipments you billed on it and how much Old Kingdom quoted for them."

Connie nodded. Her expression suggested that Katie should have said that in the first place, which she had.

The unpleasant exchange did have the side effect of completely distracting Katie from her tension. She turned away from Connie's desk oddly relaxed. "Hey, Mike," she said, "and Cameron." Talking to both of them together was a great way to appear casual. "You guys have nice weekends?"

Cameron's mouth twitched with a quick smile. He seemed to be acknowledging the polite comment more than agreeing he'd had a nice weekend. Katie felt a stab of guilt that she might have ruined his weekend with her blunt note.

"Well, I got humbled by my grandkids," Mike said.

"Sounds like a story," Katie said.

Mike glanced at Cameron, who also appeared interested in the teaser.

"Three of them wanted me to play soccer with them," Mike started. "They're eleven, nine and four. I thought it'd be most fair if I teamed up with the 4-year-old. But he said, 'No. I want Amelia on my team.' She's the 11-year-old." Mike paused to make sure they were following. Katie was following, though she was also aware of how often her eyes were flickering to Cameron to make sure he was paying more attention to Mike than to her. "So I thought I was going to have to take it easy a bit to keep it competitive. But Amelia is good. I even underestimated how fast the 4-year-old is. They beat us pretty badly."

Cameron was amused. "Did you let them think you were holding back?"

"Maybe a little," Mike said. "Not that they believed me." Mike described a few impressive moves by the kids he was clearly proud to have been humbled by while a heavyset man walked behind Katie with a stack of files.

He plopped the whole stack on the edge of Connie's desk. "Let's talk about this mess," he said.

Katie tried to focus on Mike's story, but the other man was louder.

"Are those mine?" Connie asked.

"Every single one of them is way past due, and I'm tired of trying to collect on bills I can't explain. Todd's on his way to ensure you can't just brush me off for later."

The tension was growing by the second, as was the anger in the man's voice. Katie gave a wave to Mike and Cameron and didn't worry that they didn't know why she was leaving in a hurry. She left for lunch soon after, where she thought about the possibility of Cameron showing up in a very different light.

Could she invite him to join her as a friendly coworker? If they continued to see each other through Audra, could they form a casual non-work relationship? It could get complicated if she had to remember what he told her in person and in print. But everything she already knew told her that Cameron was a really good person. He was someone she would be lucky to count as a friend. She was going to have to work at being satisfied with that.

Audra respectfully didn't bring him up during lunch, though she probably noticed that Katie was having trouble shaking her habit of watching the door. The food was still delicious.

The afternoon was boring. Home was quiet. She sat alone, thinking that she was back to square one in her pursuit of a family. Actually, it was more like negative one. She was feeling disappointed and numb and had to wait for those feelings to pass before she'd be ready to search for a new guy on Courting Catholics.

A horrible thought interrupted her melancholy. She could never post a picture on the site now, not as long as Cameron might recognize her. That was certainly going to limit the guys willing to talk to her when she was ready to respond. Did she need to wait for him to end his subscription? Worse, did she have to regularly hunt for his profile to know when he did? That wasn't going to help her move on. She might be at negative five.

Katie tossed her laptop onto the coach next to her. She got up and paced. It was past time for dinner, but she had no appetite. She checked her phone more out of restlessness than curiosity. Cecelia had her baby! There was a group text with a picture of a red-faced bundle of joy, followed by several congratulatory responses. Katie added a note of gratitude for the cute picture. She gazed at her new niece for a few moments until her eyes were too watery to see it. The dream of a family of her own had taken serious hits, and it hurt. It wasn't only the dream that hurt. She wanted to talk to Cameron so badly. She missed him.

12

Tichu was supposed to be a fun distraction. But Ryan had just asked a question that had nothing to do with Tichu and everything to do with what he wanted to be distracted from.

"No comment," Cameron said.

"I think that means he has *not* met her yet," Logan observed. He was talking to Ryan. They both paused to give Cameron a chance to correct the interpretation.

Cameron almost told them he was never going to meet her because they would stop probing if they knew things had gone south. He decided to wait to see how long it took them to move on without him saying anything.

It might help that Trevor was more interested in the game. "Whose lead is it?"

"It's mine," Ryan said. "Just thought I'd throw out a question while I decided." After a few seconds, he dropped a two on the table.

That shouldn't have taken any deliberation. And it was exactly what Cameron was waiting for. He pounced on the trick with an ace, then played a long straight to go out.

"Nice." Trevor approved because he was Cameron's partner.

The others finished quickly and Logan was shuffling two seconds after he recorded the points. "Is it my deal?" he asked.

Cameron nodded. So did Trevor. Ryan said, "So has there at least been some progress towards meeting this mysterious woman?"

There had been progress *away* from meeting her. Ryan didn't ask about backward progress. Cameron would talk about it if he thought there was any chance one of these guys could tell him what he'd done wrong. He collected the cards Logan dealt while he waited for a new subject.

"Dad wants us to come over tomorrow," Trevor said.

"Yeah." Ryan picked up a card as he answered. "He texted me, too."

"Uh, actually, he asked for my help, too," Logan said.

All three of them turned to Cameron before Ryan explained. "It's a furniture-moving party. I'm sorry you weren't invited."

"I don't think I'm sorry," Cameron said, because that didn't sound like a real party.

Trevor sighed. "It seems like about once a year our mom decides everything heavy would look better somewhere else." He frowned at his cards. It wasn't necessarily a sign of disapproval. That was his concentration face.

Cameron tried not to mimic the expression. No one needed to know that his cards deserved it. They found out through the course of the round though. He still had several left when everyone else was out. "I had a king," he said, laying the remainder on the table, "but I also had a three and a pair of sixes."

"I don't think I can blame you for not going out," Trevor said.

Logan was shuffling again. "Speaking of a pair of sixes, when did you say you were going to meet her?"

Laughter met the ridiculous segue, and even Cameron was amused by the badgering. "All right," he said. "You guys might as well know that it's over."

"Over?" Ryan echoed.

Logan handed the deck to Trevor to deal. "So the meeting went poorly?"

Trevor passed the cards from the deck slowly. It seemed that though he wasn't asking questions himself, he was happy to provide time for Cameron to give answers.

"We never met. She flat out refused and said we should stop talking."

"Ow." Ryan winced. "Sorry."

"I thought she wanted to meet," Logan said. "What happened?"

"I thought so, too." Cameron set his cards facedown on the table. "It seemed like things were going well. The chats were... fun. And we were both excited about being local and eventually moving towards a real relationship. I had asked to meet before, and she had no problem telling me she wanted more time or not yet or... then all of a sudden... boom, this won't work. I have no idea what I did."

All three of his friends shook their heads sadly as though they could relate. But there was little comfort in company. Crash and burn was still crash and burn no matter how many people were in the plane. Since there was no advice forthcoming, Cameron picked up his cards again.

Logan was checking the time a lot, which he always did when it got late enough to start expecting Audra. It reminded Cameron that there was a related topic on which he could use advice. He might as well plunge into not getting help there either.

"Before the girls get here, I wonder if I could get some... opinions."

"Before the girls get here?" Those were the only words Ryan said, but his inflection asked if the opinions were about those girls.

"Yeah, um, tell me if you notice anything about Audra's new friend, Katherine."

"Oh, the one you work with?" Logan said.

Cameron nodded.

"What are we supposed to notice?" Trevor asked.

"I don't know." Cameron shrugged. "I'm sure I'm imagining things, but I... Katherine's been at EJ longer than I have. We almost never used to talk beyond an occasional hello or just a smile and nod.

Until recently. It seems like she's maybe been making excuses to stop by my desk or... I don't know. I can't believe there's any interest there except... maybe?"

"Hmm," was Trevor's only response.

"You don't think she, uh..." Logan seemed to be hesitating to say something more than searching for the words, "that she buddied up to Audra to get over here and see you?"

"What!? No!" Cameron hadn't even considered anything like that, and now that Logan put the idea out there, it still seemed impossible. "Audra's been looking for a new Tichu fourth and there's no way Katherine could have known I was connected to her. The surprise seemed genuine. It's just that... you all know I'm reluctant to get involved with anyone at work, but if Audra likes her, that might be a sign that she's more than just a pretty face."

"So you want us to help you look for signals that some sort of move on your part would be welcome?" Ryan asked.

Cameron shrugged. That was basically what he was asking. He wasn't entirely sure he wanted to make a move though. He wondered if it would be right when he was still hoping Katie would change her mind and start messaging him again.

Trevor was wiggling the cards he wanted to pass on the table to nudge Cameron into sorting his. "You are familiar with the expression 'the blind leading the blind,' right?"

The other guys chuckled as Cameron picked up his cards. "Yeah. I know you're not experts either, but I thought maybe we could get a consensus or –" He clamped his mouth shut as the doorbell rang.

Audra led her party inside.

Alison was the last to enter, but she swept past the others to lean over and put an arm around Trevor. "Mom came to watch, and she's waiting in the truck so I need to go. I'll see you later." She stood and brushed her fingers over his hair before she waved hi and bye to the other guys.

Cameron was taking this in peripherally as he got his cards in order. As he prepared to pass, he let his eyes seek out Katherine. Their eyes locked for only a moment before hers darted away.

"Audra!" Ryan said at the same time.

Cameron couldn't tell if Katherine was avoiding his gaze or simply curious about the warning note.

Audra was stepping away from Ryan. "Why is it such a big deal if I look at your cards?"

"You know why," he said. "If you keep doing it anyway, I might have to start tilting your painting before you come over."

She gasped with feigned indignation. She knew he was kidding. But maybe her eyes didn't. They seemed to involuntarily check that the painting was straight just because it'd been mentioned.

"Oh, is this one of yours?" Katherine moved closer to the art. "It's awesome," she said.

"Thank you," Audra said.

Katherine had her back to Cameron as she admired the scene on the wall. He noticed that her shape was nice to look at, too. She had changed after work into a long sweater with leggings. She was always beautiful dressed up for work, but this casual version seemed more approachable. Now he needed to decide if that was a good idea.

She turned to face him rather suddenly. "Hey, Cameron, did David make good on his threat?"

Cameron felt his eyes rolling, which was probably good if it covered the fact that they'd been roving her. "Unfortunately, yes," he said.

"Why is that unfortunate?" Katherine pinched her lips in an expression that had recently become familiar. It had appeared several times when Mike hinted at an entertaining story. It said she was preparing a real smile, and Cameron found it more appealing when it was aimed at him.

"We *all* have to go through retraining now."

The full smile broke out as his reward. He'd expected Katherine to be amused, even though what he said wasn't that funny from his perspective.

"Wait. What's going on at work?" Audra asked.

Ryan and Logan had already set their cards down. Trevor reluctantly folded his hand as well. It seemed the game was paused to hear about the situation.

"Well, there's this woman in Cameron's department who…" Katherine grasped for a description, probably the kindest. "She just… So I go up to her and say something like, 'Your file says we expect this company to bill us this much and they're billing us this other amount. Can you explain the difference?' and she'll look at me like she doesn't understand why that matters. It wouldn't be so bad to explain things over and over if she didn't act like I'm trying to harass her by doing my job. And if she would just look it up the first time I ask, I wouldn't have to bother her nearly as often."

Cameron nodded. He'd overheard Katherine talking to Connie enough to be frustrated on her behalf. It occurred to him now how patient she always sounded when she asked about billing discrepancies. He admired the effort.

"So on Monday…" Katherine gestured to Cameron as though he should pick up the story.

He felt the eyes of everyone in the room follow her hand to him. "Okay, this guy, David, came into my office ranting at the woman Katherine is talking about. I guess she frustrates people on the receivables side, too, and he'd reached the end of his rope. He had called a VP to meet him there and said he was going to refuse to do his job until someone taught her how to do hers properly. When the VP got there, he ushered them both into a conference room to talk things out. There were a lot of closed-door meetings and a lot of gossip the next few days."

"And now you have to be retrained, too?" Ryan asked.

Cameron sighed. "Yes. There was an announcement today

that everyone in my department is going to be sitting through some seminars in the near future, though they haven't been scheduled yet. I assume it's related to David's demand though I don't know if they didn't want to single anyone out or if they discovered through all those meetings that other people were making similar mistakes."

"I'm sure the seminars will be fun," Trevor said dryly. He was fanning out his hand again so Cameron began to do the same.

When they finished the round, Audra began to dissect it for Katherine. She explained how she might have been tempted to play the aces as a pair, but Logan had made the call to save them to win two tricks. Katherine appeared to be an attentive student.

Trevor rapped his knuckles on the table, then motioned for Logan to pass the cards to the dealer.

"Oh, sorry." Logan gave the deck to Ryan. "I was listening to the commentary."

"Enjoying the praise?" Ryan asked.

"Mostly. I didn't actually hear the words 'Logan was right' at any point."

"Well, it wouldn't have worked if Ryan had played the full house before the single," Violet said. She was standing behind Ryan, who let her see his cards because she had a better poker face than his sister.

"I guess we won't be hearing anyone say 'Ryan was right' either," he said on a sigh.

Violet laughed. "Well, you didn't know what he had at the time. I wouldn't have counted on nines to win either."

Cameron picked up his cards as he listened to the banter and enjoyed watching Katherine watch it. She sent a few glances his way. But she looked at other people, too. It could have been wishful thinking on his part that her eyes were communicating hope. She and the other women left after the next round, laughing at some inside joke about cranberries.

Logan shuffled until the door closed behind them, then he set the cards in front of Cameron and said, "I don't know."

"I think it's my deal," Cameron said, because he thought that was what Logan was asking.

"I don't know about Katherine," Logan clarified. "I didn't notice any particular interest or disinterest."

Trevor and Ryan simultaneously shook their heads to indicate further lack of information. It seemed the consensus was that Cameron would have to figure it out on his own, if at all. He would have been disappointed if he'd expected anything different.

13

Cameron didn't know what had gotten into Elijah, but he had a guess and didn't mind benefiting from the sudden desire to cook. He got another text about leftovers Monday morning. That colored pencil had been dropped by a girl. Elijah picked it up as an excuse to talk to her. He'd shifted his schedule so that he was getting up earlier in the evenings and going to sleep sooner. This and the cooking practice seemed like hints that the talk had gone well.

Elijah had been making himself real dinners the last week or so and offering leftovers to Cameron in exchange for his opinion. He'd taken most of them to work for lunch. But he'd already packed a lunch Sunday night. As he reheated spaghetti and meatballs for breakfast, he wasn't sure Elijah was the one doing anything unusual. Spaghetti wasn't a bad breakfast. Cameron finished it and sent Elijah a note of thanks saying that he would have preferred the meatballs bite size so he didn't have to cut them up but the flavor was awesome.

Work was more fine than awesome. He didn't spend the whole day distracted. It was only when he heard someone coming through the door that he wondered if Katherine might show up in his office. Yet somehow he wasn't paying attention when she actually appeared. He was studying a form when he realized that Mike was laughing at something she'd said. Cameron wished he'd heard whatever it was.

"Hi, Katherine," he said. "I didn't see you come in."

"Told you he was focused," Mike said.

Katherine smiled. "Did you win?"

"What?" Cameron looked at his paperwork in confusion.

"Tichu," Katherine said. "You and Trevor were behind when I left on Friday."

"Oh, yeah. We were *more* behind after you left."

She offered a sympathetic nod.

"You two getting together on the weekends?" Mike asked.

"No." Katherine answered very quickly. Was she repulsed by the suggestion or honestly squelching rumors? "We just bumped into each other as we discovered that a friend of mine is the sister of two of his friends."

Mike nodded and said, "Small world."

A shift in Katherine's stance hinted that she was about to head back to her own office. Cameron felt a sudden urge to keep her there longer. "Did you notice what day it is?"

Her eyes drifted into space as she became thoughtful. And didn't leave.

"It's Monday," Cameron said. With two seconds to think, his conversation starter was lame. But she didn't leave.

She gave a hint of a smile, as though preparing to laugh at the joke she didn't yet get. "That I know," she said. "Is there a holiday or something?"

"No. Or not one that I know of. But on Friday you asked if we were ready for the weekend so I think now you're supposed to sarcastically ask if we're glad to be back at work."

"Right." Katherine let out a one-syllable laugh but didn't quite get any sarcasm in her voice before she asked, "Are you?"

At the moment, Cameron was in fact very glad to be where he was. "Well, I can definitely think of worse places to be," he said. Then he looked at Mike to include him in the question.

"I agree there are worse places," Mike said. "I do wish our workday started earlier though."

"Earlier?" Katherine sounded mildly surprised but mostly just interested in his reasoning.

"I know you young people probably want to sleep in, but I'm an early riser." Mike shifted a few papers around as he spoke. "By the time I come here, I've been up for a few hours trying to decide which projects I can squeeze in first. It'd be nice if I could come to work pretty much as soon as I'm dressed in the morning, then come home that much earlier. Otherwise, it kind of feels like it's splitting my day."

"I think I can see that," Katherine said. She gave an understanding nod. "I wouldn't want the day to start earlier or later though. I've kind of tailored my mornings around the 8 o'clock start time. If it changed, I'd be frazzled trying to figure out new routines."

"I'd just set my alarm for a different time," Cameron said, wishing he had something more interesting – or just interesting – to add.

Katherine gave them both a smile and a see you later before she walked out. Cameron resisted the impulse to turn and watch her, lest anyone misinterpret a desire to see her a few more seconds for a desire to watch her walk.

He focused on his work until he got home and had little else to think about. He could fruitlessly wonder how he'd messed things up with Katie. He could nurse the guilt about turning down a dinner invitation from his mom. He'd used Elijah's cooking kick as a reason he didn't need to be fed, even though he hadn't eaten any of Elijah's meals at dinnertime. Cameron hadn't visited his parents since Katie dropped him. His mom would ask, and he didn't want to talk about it when he didn't know any of the answers to any of the questions.

That left him with the image of Katherine's slightly wide-eyed expression when she mentioned rearranging her morning routines as the most enjoyable thought in his head. Something about that worried look touched a protective instinct. Though it was absurd to think of protecting her from her own exacting schedule. Katherine was a smart, competent woman though. That hint of vulnerability suggested that maybe she didn't have to be one hundred percent independent, that maybe she was looking for someone to lean on from time to time, and maybe she was even looking in his direction.

And maybe Cameron was running with an idea more dangerous than scissors. Her next visit to his office couldn't in any way be construed as an excuse to see him. She was sent by her boss.

Katherine came into the room and did not immediately approach Connie's desk. She grabbed a chair from an unused desk and wheeled it into position next to Cameron's desk and Mike's. She sat down with a notebook in her lap and looked between them expectantly.

"I feel as though I'm about to be interviewed," Mike said.

"Sort of. If you guys have a few minutes to talk to me, that is." Katherine lifted her eyebrows in question.

"Sure." Cameron set down his pen. "What's up?"

"I can come back if you're busy," Katherine said, looking at Mike.

"Nonsense," he said. "You got me curious what this is all about now."

"A little bird told me there's going to be some, uh, continuing education opportunities offered in the near future. I'm on a fact-finding mission about that."

"I think you'll find that whether or not we need the *opportunity* is more a matter of opinion than fact," Mike observed.

"Hey! Are you going to be leading the payables seminar?" Cameron knew his voice betrayed his hope. It would be less horrible to sit through if Katherine was doing the talking.

She was still smiling at the truth of what Mike had said so he couldn't tell if she was happy that he cared who was leading. She glanced around the room and lowered her voice. "It's possible that someone suggested I do it, and I was able to flatter that someone into believing he would do a better job."

Mike chuckled.

Cameron didn't think it was all that funny. He could easily picture Katherine turning a guy into putty with a pretty smile and an ego pat. The same tactics had once gotten him to believe a lot of things that weren't true.

"But I still have to do the research," Katherine said. She tapped her notebook. "I have a list of our biggest accounts. I need to find out some standard procedures from you guys. Um... which ones give you verbal quotes versus written, whether you talk to the same person each time, how you record stuff... that sort of thing."

"Sounds like we get to educate you," Mike said.

Katherine smiled at him. "I would not be disappointed to learn something."

Cameron could see her sincerity as she began her list. She made notes and nodded appreciatively as she gathered information. Though she was thoroughly professional, she kept the tone light and wasn't as intimidating as she seemed at times. It was an enjoyable conversation about very mundane things. When she got up and thanked them for their time, Cameron was surprised at how much time he'd given her. He realized that Mike had chimed in occasionally but had mostly let Cameron do the talking. Given that Mike had a lot of seniority, his respect was as valuable as Katherine's attention.

But did her interest go beyond business? That was a question that was quickly becoming urgent. If it did, Cameron needed to start learning more about her – the real her – before he became too infatuated. And if it didn't, he needed to stop thinking about her altogether. Either way, he needed to pray hard for some help.

She was wearing his favorite dress the next time he saw her, and that didn't help. It was black with little red flowers and a ruffle along the bottom. Cameron didn't have the vocabulary to really describe the dress other than it looked amazing on Katherine. He tried to see as much as he could out of the side of his eye as she discussed some confusing numbers with Connie.

When she turned, he was internally stumbling over words he couldn't get out of his mouth. He wanted to say something about how nice she looked, something that might give her an excuse to stop and chat if she was hoping for an excuse. But nothing could get past "wow."

"Katherine, you look very nice today," Mike said.

Cameron kicked himself. That should not have been difficult to come up with.

It did make Katherine stop to thank Mike. A light blush spread across her face as she glanced at Cameron. He realized that it might have something to do with the fact that he was nodding like a bobblehead at the sentiment.

"I assume you're looking forward to your game tonight?" she asked Cameron.

"Yes," he said, making a concerted effort to hold his head steady with the word.

"What about you, Katherine?" Mike said. "Any exciting plans for the weekend?"

"Actually, yes." Her entire face lit up to confirm it. "My sister had a baby last weekend, and she's *finally* letting me come over after work today to meet her. I get to spend a little time snuggling with a newborn before I meet up with friends. It'll be a good night."

Mike nodded. "I take it this is her first baby?"

"What gave it away?" Katherine asked, though her tone hinted that she already knew the answer.

"Most experienced moms don't wait a week before they let family come over to help."

"I'm not sure how much help it'll be to let me hold the baby for a half hour."

Mike sat back in his chair. "According to my wife and all three of my daughters-in-law, the best thing you can do is tell her she can nap while you hold the baby so she doesn't feel the need to entertain you."

Katherine nodded thoughtfully. "I thought you were going to tell me to make sure I say her baby is the cutest one I've ever seen."

"That wouldn't hurt," Mike said with a laugh.

Cameron had nothing to contribute to the conversation and yet they both looked to include him right then. After he stared back for a few moments, Mike asked if he had any nieces or nephews.

"No siblings," Cameron said.

"Oh. Your parents are looking at you as the only hope for grandkids," Mike said knowingly. "Any pressure yet?"

"Not yet." The observation did make Cameron wonder if his mom's questions about a significant woman in his life would eventually morph into questions about when the kids would come.

"That's better than, uh…" Katherine bit her lower lip against what she'd almost said.

Cameron wanted to encourage her to finish the thought, but she seemed uncomfortable. He didn't know if he should say anything. Mike appeared similarly uncertain.

Katherine took pity and didn't make anyone ask. "I was going to say," she said, "that I kind of wish my parents would bug me about grandkids because when they don't say anything, and I'm thirty, it kind of feels like they've given up on me."

His eyebrows probably didn't give him away, but Cameron wasn't entirely sure he'd covered his surprise. He knew Katherine was older because she'd also been hired after college at least a year before him. He would have guessed twenty-five or twenty-six though. Age was a strike against her being interested in him. She likely thought he was too young. There wasn't time to dwell on it because Katherine immediately diverted them to a new subject.

"Mike, you didn't tell us if you have any fun plans for the weekend."

"Because I don't," he said. "One of the older grandkids is coming over – Amelia – because my wife offered to help make a Halloween costume. It's based on a character in a book with no pictures, but I know Amelia has a very specific picture in her head, and my wife will try to make it fit one of her patterns, and it's going to be hard to watch them clash. Plus, it's too early to be thinking about Halloween anyway."

"You're right," Katherine said. "That does not sound like a lot of fun. But speaking of fun, I should get back to my office."

Cameron returned her smile as she walked away wishing he knew if he had a chance. He wasn't a teenager anymore. He could go in with his eyes open and not ignore things that made them a poor match and... well, probably make things awkward at work when he failed to win her over. But he'd survived worse, and Katherine was beginning to seem like someone who was worth the risk. He only needed some sort of sign that she was open to the risk.

She had barely left the room when Mike pushed his chair against the front of Cameron's desk. He leaned forward and dropped his voice to a whisper. "I'm pretty sure she's not stopping by to talk to *me*."

Cameron jumped from his chair and moved to the hallway as fast as he could without actually running. Katherine must have been walking slowly. She wasn't very far ahead. She hadn't looked back. He could still chicken out. Mike had been married for almost forty years though. It was possible he knew something.

"Hey, Katherine, wait a sec."

Her steps jerked slightly as she came to a stop and faced him with her eyes wide.

He'd just chased her into the hallway so of course she was startled. He closed the gap and plowed ahead because chasing her for no reason might be creepier. "I wanted to ask if you'd be willing to get together sometime outside of work. I mean, I know you're busy tonight, but maybe tomorrow? Could we have dinner or something?"

Katherine appeared speechless. He wasn't sure she'd blinked the whole time he was talking, though babbling was more like it. The surprise must mean she had not been trying to get his attention, that Mike was as clueless about women as everyone else he knew. Cameron was trying to decide if he needed to apologize or just say never mind or…

"Yes," Katherine said suddenly. "There's a place in Andauk that makes really good burgers. Do you like burgers?"

Cameron nodded. She'd said yes. He would have nodded at whatever she said next, which was not a healthy beginning. But once his brain had a few seconds to recover from the elation of not being rejected, he could honestly say he did like hamburgers. No harm done.

"Great. It's called Burger Brothers," Katherine said. "What time should we meet?"

"6 o'clock?"

She nodded, smiled nervously, and hurried down the hallway.

Cameron walked very slowly in the opposite direction. His office was only about ten steps away and he needed every one of them to wipe the goofy grin off his face. After he sat down, Mike sent him an expectant glance. Cameron returned it with a quick thumbs up.

14

The new baby was not a disappointment. She was as cute and tiny and precious as Katie expected. Cecelia was generous in letting Katie hold her almost as soon as she arrived, and without giving much instruction about how to do it properly. But the warm bundle didn't do much to calm the storm of thoughts churning through Katie's head. It only relaxed her enough to want to talk to someone about those thoughts, and Cecelia was right there.

Katie had offered to let her nap. But Cecelia's husband, Nick, had two weeks off work and had been insisting she get tons of rest. She looked pretty perky. And as soon as they were settled, Cecelia demanded an update on the online dating.

"You said yet at some point," she said. "You told me you hadn't met anyone in person *yet*, which means you were at least talking to someone you might meet. Tell me something about him."

"I'm not sure where to start," Katie said.

Cecelia rolled her eyes. "What's his name?"

"Cameron."

"How long have you been sending him messages?"

"A few months."

"And you haven't met him!?" Cecelia sounded exasperated, then had a different thought. "Wait. Does he live far away? Are you moving?"

Katie sighed at her sister jumping so suddenly to the idea of her moving. "He doesn't live far away," she said. "And we have already met. But he doesn't know that. Yet."

Cecelia gasped and leaned forward. "This sounds good." She gestured for Katie to start spilling details.

Katie paused because she knew that Cecelia would share everything she said with everyone in the family unless she specifically asked her not to. It felt childish to hide it. Though she wasn't thrilled about letting everyone know immediately, Katie resigned herself to that fate. If things actually worked out with Cameron, they would all know the story eventually. And if it didn't work out, she'd feel worse about that than about anyone knowing.

"Okay," Katie said. "I'm going to tell you because I need advice." She told pretty much the same story she told Audra about how she thought she was going to get a peek at the online guy and saw someone she knew from work. But now there were the new details about how she'd ended the online part rather than be rejected in person. And how he'd just surprised her by asking her out.

"Wow!" Cecelia smiled big. "This is exciting. You're having dinner with him tomorrow?"

"Yes."

"And you're going to tell him everything?"

"This is where I need advice," Katie said.

Cecelia narrowed her eyes threateningly. "You *have* to tell him."

"Oh, I know." She would have said that if Cecelia hadn't interrupted. "But I can't decide if I should write to him to explain I'm the same person from work or if I should wait until I get there and explain I'm the same person from the site."

"Oh." Cecelia sounded confused and stopped looking at Katie as though she was a moron.

"I think I could give a more thorough explanation in writing," Katie said. "I'm afraid I'll be so nervous in person that I'll leave stuff out or make it sound like I was trying to hide or… But I feel like I owe him an apology for ending the online thing so abruptly and with no explanation. Does that mean he deserves to hear it right from me? Writing feels like the easy way, and I owe him the hard way. But only if it's hard for me. And what if he blocked my account after I ticked him off, and I go to the date not knowing if he got my explanation at all?"

"Hmm." Cecelia nodded as she appeared to mull over the choices. "I think we need a guy's opinion. Nick!"

Katie jumped at the sudden increase in volume. She was relieved when the sleeping baby in her arms continued to sleep. She was not comforted that the sound of footsteps on the stairs meant her embarrassing story was going to begin to spread only a minute after she told it.

"What do you need?" Nick asked as soon as he got to the bottom of the stairs. He was wearing shorts and a t-shirt – though it was in Katie's opinion too chilly for shorts – and looked as though he hadn't shaved since the baby came. He had light hair with a reddish tint that didn't show up as much in the early beard. It seemed he had dropped everything to respond to his wife's summons without literally dropping anything. There was a pink plastic flower in one of his hands and a screwdriver in the other. A burp rag hung from one shoulder.

His slightly comical appearance distracted Cecelia. "What were you doing?" she asked.

He waved the flower. "I'm trying to put this thing together."

"She's not going to be able to use that for at least a few months."

"I know," he said. "I want to do as much as I can before I have to go back to work."

"Do you plan on working twenty-four hours a day?"

"No, but I'll be busier, and I have time now. Plus, there is a chance it'll take me months to get this together because the diagram isn't making any sense."

Cecelia laughed at the exaggeration. "I'm glad it sounds like you need a break because we need your opinion on something."

"Shoot," he said.

"You know Katie's been trying to find someone through the Catholic dating site."

Nick nodded, but his eyes darted up the stairs as though now that he knew the subject he would rather go back and wrestle with tiny screws and confusing directions.

"Well, she's been talking to someone and she found out that it's actually someone she works with and they have a date this weekend. Should she tell him before the date or do it in person?"

"How did you find out who he is without him finding out who you are?" Nick asked.

"That's kind of a long story," Katie said, because he probably wanted to hear it less than she wanted to tell it. And Cecelia would give him the details later anyway.

Nick nodded gratefully. He glanced up the stairs again. "I'm not sure I want to get involved with this."

Cecelia sighed at him. "Giving an opinion is not getting involved. Just tell us if you were the guy, how would you prefer to find out?"

He scratched his head. With the screwdriver. "I guess I'd say you should tell him before the date to level the playing field. It seems kind of unfair for him to show up knowing less than you."

"That's what I was thinking," Cecelia said.

"Then why did you ask me?" Nick said.

"Because you're a guy. You might have had a different perspective. Plus, the more people agree, the more convincing we are."

Nick frowned and started back up the stairs.

"Nick?" Cecelia called.

He stopped and turned back.

"Do you know that you're still wearing a burp rag?"

He looked at his shoulder, then pulled the rag off and threw it at his wife before he continued his retreat.

Katie was laughing. Nick and Cecelia were good together.

Cecelia neatly folded the rag and set it next to her as she resumed the conversation with her sister. "So you're going to write Cameron a letter tonight telling him everything, then you have dinner on Saturday. When do you bring him over for the family to meet?"

"Never," Katie said.

Cecelia just laughed and waited for the real answer.

"I'm not sure he'll even show up on Saturday after I tell him who I am." Katie wasn't trying to be pessimistic, just bracing for different outcomes. "I wouldn't blame him. I may not have... I didn't intentionally mislead him about anything. But it is my fault that we talked so long before..." It was difficult to explain without admitting how she'd delayed the meeting to continue her crush-induced fantasies. Her conscience understood that she'd done something wrong even if dishonest wasn't the exact word for it.

"Of course he'll show up," Cecelia said. "I bet he'll be happy to find out."

"To find out that I sort of tricked him?"

"You didn't trick anybody. It's just... a coincidence." Her eyes sparkled as an idea hit her. "Oh, you guys are going to have the cutest how we met story ever!"

Katie tried to spend a few minutes soaking up the peace of a newborn in her arms because none of Cecelia's confidence was rubbing off on her. And first she had to get through the evening. She was going to see Cameron with his friends. She was sure it would be better to confess her secret identity after the Tichu night so he could have time alone to think about it. But the longer she waited, the greater the chance he would be angry that she waited. Would he tell anyone they had a date the next day? Would it seem like she was hiding something if he mentioned it? She was now.

Cecelia made Katie promise to text her when she got home Saturday night. Then if she was awake, she would call for full details. Katie didn't think it was fair to ask her anything when the baby had her all mushy and weak, but now that Cecelia knew what was going on, it was probably better to keep her updated so she didn't spread speculation that people could confuse with facts.

Katie had stopped at home to change before she was introduced to the new niece so she was able to go straight to Audra's afterwards. She enjoyed the game and the new painting Audra showed everyone. Alison was thrilled that a customer wanted her to carve some designs in a table's legs. She usually only got to do designs with paint. That part of the evening was fun and fast.

Time began to crawl the moment Violet said they should visit the guys. Katie was last in the single-file line around the house. She was determined to be completely casual and nonchalant if there was any mention of what she or Cameron had planned the next day and maybe it wouldn't come up.

Audra had already let herself in by the time Katie turned the corner. She watched Violet disappear through the open door, and then Alison. Katie reminded herself to breathe as she crossed the threshold. It shouldn't be any harder than last week and certainly not more stressful than when she found out the two Camerons were the same guy. But her feelings weren't just uncertainty, they were guilty uncertainty.

Knowing something he didn't know seemed fine when it seemed he wouldn't want to know. She'd been so sure she'd be rejected that she thought she was doing him a favor by avoiding the actual rejecting. Now that he expressed interest, he needed to know. Every minute she didn't tell him felt like a serious lie of omission. Was she rationalizing the delay or would he want her to wait until after the game? She was positive he wouldn't want to be told in front of a room full of people so it was too late to change her mind.

The scene in Trevor and Ryan's apartment was not what Katie expected. Rather than trying to decide the correct amount of eye contact with Cameron to appear nervous but not deceptive and happy but not happy about hiding something, she was faced with three confused women. Cameron and the other guys weren't there at all. Tichu cards sat in four piles on the table, one with three cards lined up to pass.

"Trevor? Ryan?" Audra called out and looked down a hallway that presumably led to their bedrooms.

"This is weird," Alison said. "They must have left very suddenly."

Audra picked up a phone from the table. "They are definitely in the middle of a game," she said as she set it back down. "I'll text my brothers."

"Is there any chance they left because they knew we were coming?" Violet asked.

"Like to surprise us?" Alison glanced into the kitchen as though someone might be hiding in there. She looked doubtful though.

Violet shrugged. She didn't seem convinced of her own idea.

Katie was thinking of asking if they should leave. She wasn't feeling as disappointed as the other women appeared. This was a chance to run home and start that letter without seeing Cameron first. She wasn't able to suggest leaving – in vague terms of having things to do anyway – before the door opened behind her, and the four missing guys entered.

Trevor was in the lead. "Intruders," he said. "I should have locked the door."

His joke gave Katie a reason to smile at Cameron, who came in next. He returned the smile and reclaimed his seat at the table. It was the one that happened to be facing Katie, and the one with cards ready to pass.

Ryan and Logan came in talking about something that sounded sports related.

"Where were you guys?" Audra asked.

Logan started laughing.

Ryan gave him a friendly shove as they grabbed chairs.

"Why don't you tell them?" Trevor nodded at Ryan.

Ryan only said, "It was there," while he fanned out his cards.

That made Logan laugh again.

"Is someone going to tell us what's so funny?" Audra said.

Katie couldn't help stealing glances at Cameron, who was doing the same in her direction. A smile kept twitching the corners of his mouth. She couldn't tell if part of it came from being happy to see her or if he was solely amused by whatever made the other guys laugh.

Logan gave in to Audra's plea. "Your brothers were having the most ridiculous argument. Did you notice the construction down at the corner? I think they were replacing the curb or something."

"That's the way I go to work," Audra said, "so, yeah, I noticed having to drive around the construction."

"Well, I guess they finished up three or four days ago," Logan continued, "and Ryan thought they left a cone behind."

"They did," Ryan said.

"He said something about it as we were getting started tonight, but Trevor accused him of imagining things."

"He was," Trevor said at the same time Ryan said, "I didn't."

"He wouldn't let it go, kept saying things like, 'Don't imagine you have the dragon,' or 'Those are twos not an orange cone,' until Ryan finally said we needed to go down there and settle it."

"So you guys just got back from walking to the corner to see the cone?" Alison asked.

Trevor smiled at her. "That wasn't there."

"It wasn't?" Violet looked at Audra as though they both knew something.

Katie was still kind of lost. Being distracted by trying not to look at Cameron more than anyone else wasn't helping. Though he was quiet, his eyes said he was entertained by the story, and keeping up with it.

"So it didn't settle anything," Logan said. "There was no cone, but Ryan still insists one was left behind and was there this morning."

"It was," Audra said.

"I saw it, too," Violet added.

Ryan pointed a finger between them and said, "Witnesses!"

"You're both taking his side?" Trevor asked.

"We're not taking sides," Audra said. She rolled her eyes at Trevor in a way that clearly indicated she was not taking *his* side. "We're just being honest. I know Violet saw it because we were just talking about it last night. Not a big discussion or anything, but I asked if she'd noticed the leftover cone and then we wondered if someone from the town would pick it up before some kid decided it was abandoned and fair game. Then we joked about a few places a bright orange cone would look nice in our apartment."

"Sounds like a big discussion to me," Trevor mumbled.

Violet was nodding along with Audra. "Because we had talked about it, I specifically looked to see if it was still there this morning, and it was. But it wasn't there when I came home from work."

"Awesome. You're an even more reliable witness than I am." Ryan's comment was directed at Violet.

Audra glanced between them and seemed to be wondering why she wasn't getting the same credit.

"If you guys had come over a few minutes earlier," Logan said, "you could have saved us a trip."

"A little exercise never hurt anyone," Audra said.

"How about this idea?" Trevor slapped a few cards against the table as he spoke. "How about we stop talking about traffic cones and get back to the game?"

"I think someone is being a sore loser." Audra spoke under her breath to Katie.

Trevor evidently heard because he narrowed his eyes at Audra enough to say that he'd heard.

"Well, as riveting as this has been," Alison said, "I'm going to take off now." She bid farewell to the room at large but had eyes only for Trevor.

Silence fell in Alison's wake as the guys focused on Tichu. Audra was positioned behind Logan to watch his cards as he played, and Violet took up a similar stance behind Ryan. Because those two guys were sitting next to each other, Katie could stand between Audra and Violet without feeling too awkward. She watched the progress of the game until she felt Audra's elbow in her ribs. When she turned to see what that was about, Audra's eyes slid towards Cameron and back.

He was simply playing the game – and Katie knew that without having it pointed out – so there didn't seem to be anything Audra was trying to get her to notice. Was there something she wanted her to do? Impossible. Audra had been disappointed at Katie's decision to end communication with him rather than admit her identity, but there was no way she would expect her to say something right here in front of everyone. Katie tried to calmly show her confusion.

Audra was clearly annoyed. She moved her pointed gaze to Violet, widened her eyes, then dipped her chin down and up. Katie didn't know if she was supposed to try to interpret that or if it was a new message intended for Violet. She turned to Violet in time to catch the end of a head shake with a warning look. Apparently, Violet did not approve of the message. But then Audra's shoulders slumped under a thoroughly exasperated expression.

Ryan started laughing. "Give it up, sis. Your friends don't know what your weird faces mean any more than I do."

"You weren't supposed to know," Audra said. She sounded as though she was mentally stomping her foot. Or at least thinking about it.

"What are you doing?" Logan turned around to face Audra as he played his last cards. "You aren't trying to tell them what's in my hand, are you?"

"It had nothing to do with your cards," Audra said. "Exactly."

"What does exactly mean?" Logan asked.

Cameron played his final card and looked up at Katie and shared a smile at the commotion.

She tried to keep it casual on the surface, but the way her heart picked up speed could be accurately described as the opposite of casual. Trevor started talking and gave her an excuse to break the eye contact quickly.

He tossed his remaining cards towards Ryan. "I don't think I care what you guys are talking about, but I don't want to be in the dark if it *is* about the game."

"Fine." Audra exhaled audibly. "I was just trying to suggest to Katherine that since Violet and I were watching you two play," she waved a hand between the guys she meant, "that she could step around the table to see from Cameron's perspective."

Katie was relieved to find out that it was about the game. "Why didn't you just say that?" she asked.

"Because sometimes these guys are ridiculously protective of their cards. I didn't want to put Cameron on the spot to give you permission to peek. I thought it'd be better if you moved more subtly."

"You standing there making faces is not subtle," Ryan said.

"I wasn't making faces," Audra insisted. "I was making some discreet gestures."

Ryan bugged out his eyes. "This is not a discreet gesture."

"That's not what I did!"

Violet was trying so hard not to laugh that she snorted before she said, "That is kind of what you looked like."

"Thank you," Ryan said.

"How did I miss you doing that?" Trevor tipped his head as he questioned his sister.

Before she could reply, Ryan said, "Maybe because you don't pay enough attention to your surroundings."

"Oh, no," Logan moaned. "He's going to bring up the cone again."

"How does anyone not notice repeatedly driving past something that is fluorescent orange?"

"I was being sarcastic when I asked Audra that," Trevor said. "She knows I was deliberately *not* looking at her so her face didn't give away Logan's hand."

"And what exactly were you worried things on the side of the road might tell you?" Logan asked.

Audra playfully punched Logan's arm. "Now who's talking about the cone?"

"That was a valid point. And I didn't actually use the word... um, that word." Logan had been shuffling while he talked. He held up the deck and looked around to see who wanted to claim the deal.

Cameron reached for the cards and said, "I don't mind."

Katie understood that he was giving her permission to watch him play. This was somewhat impressive given that he hadn't looked at her, the conversation had been carried away from that suggestion, and there were more important things she wished he would say he didn't mind. And those things were forefront in her mind.

Audra quickly launched into a description of a new scene she wanted to paint – something with wheat and one ear of corn to make it kooky – and effectively prevented anyone who wasn't keeping up from asking Cameron what he meant. Katie felt this was intentional. She didn't know if Audra was trying to help her avoid an awkward moment or only wanted to keep the other guys from saying anything about looking at cards in general. Regardless, Katie was able to use the distraction to wait until Cameron had dealt all the cards, then move behind him with actual subtly. She found that despite the proximity, she was more relaxed when she couldn't see Cameron's eyes.

The women stayed for two more hands with occasional banter before making their exit for the night. Audra paused just before closing the door and said, "By the way, everyone, my poker face is fine."

A chorus of male laughter matched the female smiles. But Katie knew she wouldn't be smiling later. She hadn't gotten to the difficult part of the night.

15

It was nearly 1:30 AM before Katie was satisfied with her letter to Cameron. It got even later while she debated whether to send it right away or wait until it was really morning. She'd told Cameron that getting consistent sleep was one of the ways she took care of herself. Would he see the vulnerability behind the late message, how important it was to her? Or would he think sleep was one more thing she lied about?

Maybe he wouldn't even notice the time stamp. She was pretty sure he would but even more sure that she couldn't delay any longer.

*Cameron,*
*I'm sorry I ended our communication so abruptly. I hope you*
*will forgive me. Please, at least read my entire explanation*
*before you decide if you can. It may take me awhile to get it*
*all out.*

*My full name is Katherine Byrne. I know now that you will*
*recognize that name. But I didn't when we started writing. I*
*swear I didn't. This was never meant to be any kind of*
*deception. Part of the reason I backed out was that I was*
*afraid it would look like a trick.*

*I signed up as Katie because that's what most of my family*
*calls me. I figured if I was hoping to find someone who*
*would eventually become part of my family, I should*
*introduce myself the way he'd hear it all the time. I go by*

Katherine at work because that name was on my official paperwork when I started. An enthusiastic woman from HR (who I think left before you started) went around introducing me to everyone as Katherine, and I didn't care enough to correct her. I just got used to it. I promise I wasn't trying to hide behind a different name.

This is how I found out who you are. You probably don't remember, but you mentioned in one of your messages that you liked a place called the January Café. I went there for lunch to check it out. Quite a few times actually. It's embarrassing to admit, but I'm trying to be totally honest so you'll believe me. I hoped I could get a peek at you before we met. I kept coming back to watch for guys who matched your description. That's part of why I kept stalling. It was shallow and selfish, but I got kind of obsessed with the idea of... well, cheating. It would have been cheating to see you ahead of time. I have no excuse for that. But you asked why I was afraid. You deserve to know that the only thing I was afraid of was not getting what I wanted. Then I started talking to Audra. She was so friendly and gave me a reason to keep coming back and hoping I ran into you unaware.

Audra eventually invited me to join her for Tichu. I couldn't believe I found someone else who knew the game. It was a loophole. She asked me on Thursday, and it was so hard not to tell you I was going to see the cards without looking anything up. I planned to surprise you with my new knowledge and make you guess how I found out. But while we were playing the game, Audra happened to mention the names of her brothers. I knew that couldn't be a coincidence. Then she told me we were going to visit them playing next door. I thought I would get my chance to cheat after all. Maybe. It happened so fast. I wondered if you might guess who I was.

When I walked into the room and saw you were the same Cameron I worked with, I panicked. I was too shocked to do anything but want to hide. I worried about making things awkward at work. I worried Audra would be mad if I

*disrupted her Friday routine. I just panicked about
everything. That's why I tried to shut this down and
disappear.*

*You changed that by trying to shift our work relationship away
from work. Now I have to come clean. I have to catch you up
and let you know what I know. You can decide where we go
from here. I will understand if I don't hear from you this way
again. I will understand if you don't show up on Saturday. I
won't say anything at work about this. But even though I'll do
my best to make it easy on you, I think you should know that
I'll be disappointed if we have no future. Maybe you can tell
that I've missed you. Maybe that's what made you approach
me at work. I couldn't stop myself from trying to talk to you.*
   *Katie*

Though writing out her thoughts kept her up, Katie slept
surprisingly well once the message had been sent. She was still
nervous about Cameron's reaction. Nerves weren't as sleep-stealing
as a nagging conscience though.

Katie had breakfast with her laptop sitting on the table across
from her. She imagined that Cameron was in its place. What would
he say? Was there any hope he'd be happy to learn her identity? Had
he invested enough in the online relationship to be glad for the
opportunity to move forward offline? He did ask her out, the real-
life version of her. Could that combine with their chemistry in print
to form something solid? Or would the discovery feel like too much
dishonesty to handle?

A sudden fear shook Katie. What if Cameron hadn't meant to
ask her out at all? What if he was being friendly, and she
misinterpreted? How embarrassing would it be to spill her heart and
then find out he only wanted to get along better while they played
Tichu? She told herself it should only be embarrassing for Cameron.
Because it definitely sounded like he was asking her out. If she
misinterpreted, it was his fault.

Indignation felt enough like courage that she grabbed the computer and checked for messages. Nothing yet. She refused to be disappointed. It was still somewhat early on a Saturday. Cameron had no reason to expect a message. Her chance of forgiveness was better if he spent some time thinking over everything rather than write a knee-jerk reply. Katie would have no trouble thinking of excuses all day if she had to. She continued to check on and off. She was worried about finding a note that told her to go away but was convinced that going to Burger Brothers wondering whether or not he'd be there would be worse.

By midmorning, whether or not Cameron would show up was the only thing Katie did know. He responded with a note that said he was still coming. It didn't say anything else. He didn't say he was looking forward to it. He didn't say he wanted an opportunity to yell at her in person. It was four cryptic words long. What Katie really didn't know was what happened to her afternoon.

She had read the short, uninformative message a few times, then pushed it away wondering how to *not* spend the entire afternoon thinking about it. She decided to try some Lectio Divina. She knew praying with the Scriptures would be difficult with the distraction of uncertainty hovering at her elbow. But she remembered something she'd read about the importance of praying with distractions. If there was no peaceful presence felt, if there was no immediately perceived benefit of prayer, then all the efforts went to God. She liked that idea.

Katie knew she had paused for lunch. She only remembered being eager to get back to her reading, which had somehow taken up the rest of the afternoon. God had given her peace when she didn't think he could. But now that it was time to leave, the anxiety came rushing back. It followed her out the door and rode in the car telling her the drive was too short. She would be about fifteen minutes early. That was her plan. She thought that getting there first would somehow be better.

Burger Brothers was crowded at dinnertime on a Saturday. Katie quickly stepped to the side and scanned the area by the door, then the people in line and at the tables. No sign of Cameron. She let out the breath she'd held as she entered. Movement drew her attention as an older woman in a red-and-white striped dress zipped towards her on lime green roller skates.

"Howdy," the woman said. "You look new. I'm Paula. You're welcome to get in line or you can have a seat if you'd like me to bring you something."

"Thank you," Katie said. The onslaught of speed and color made anything more specific than general friendliness, which was always appreciated, difficult to process. "I… uh… am I in the way here? I'm meeting someone."

"Oh, honey, you can stand right there until your friend gets here." Paula gestured towards the counter at the back. "Chip gets a little rare when people mess with his line, and you don't want to see that."

Katie nodded. She had no idea what the woman just said but couldn't help agreeing. Chip appeared to be the name of the scarier brother who was currently taking orders. The man had dark hair with gray specks and a moustache with the purpose of hiding whether or not he was smiling.

Paula smiled broadly though and said, "Flag me down if you need anything," before she skated away.

Still no Cameron out the big front window. Katie looked around the inside again. He definitely wasn't there. But a lot of people were. Would there be a place for Katie and Cameron to eat? Only a few tables were empty, but the next customer took his food to go.

Cameron was suddenly beside her. "Hi," he said.

It knocked Katie's nerves into high gear. She was probably sweating. "Hi," she said. She smiled on the outside and cringed on the inside, knowing it must look like one of those terrible forced smiles in all the pictures she'd deleted.

Cameron sort of nodded and sort of looked at the ground. He seemed at least somewhat nervous, which did nothing to help Katie's nerves. He waved a hand towards the line. "Should we order?"

"Yeah. Yeah, okay." Katie moved with him to join the back of the line.

The place was far from silent. Music played in the background, quiet enough that Katie couldn't make out much more than a beat. It sounded like bluegrass. Voices chattered and laughed around them. No conversations raised above the others or covered the fact that she and Cameron weren't saying anything. He was staring straight ahead. Before Katie could worry he was ignoring her, she realized he was reading the menu posted above the register.

She knew he was smart. Of course it was a good idea to know what they wanted before they got to the front of the line. It was moving quickly, and she'd been warned not to mess with the line. When the guy in front of them stepped aside, Cameron gestured for Katie to order first and said, "I'm buying."

The authoritative tone suggested that an argument would be insulting. But letting him pay when she felt she owed him seemed wrong, too. Katie wrestled with indecision for a few seconds before she noticed the eyes of the mustached guy boring into her. No need to add finding out what a little rare meant to the already stressful situation. Katie said, "I'll have the Special Swiss Burger but with no mustard, please."

Chip's eyes widened ever so slightly. The mouth remained disguised. Though he seemed stoic, Katie thought she read disbelief, impatience and annoyance all at once. She figured she was imagining it because a simple order couldn't possibly provoke that kind of reaction. He hadn't entered the order though. Was he waiting for something? Oh, right.

"No fries," Katie added, "but a glass of water, please." She moved back to indicate Cameron's turn.

"Hi," he said to Chip.

Chip watched him expectantly.

"Standard Burger with fries and a Coke, please."

Chip punched a few buttons while he muttered something under his breath that sounded like, "Thank you for being able to read." He gave the total and Cameron paid.

Tension seemed to build as they waited for the burgers and took them to a table. The woman on skates bumped the edge of the table as they sat down and asked if they had everything they needed. Cameron nodded at her. He made a Sign of the Cross and silently asked God to bless his food while Katie did the same, including a plea for the night to go well. Cameron's expression revealed delight at his first bite. When he'd swallowed enough to talk, he said, "This is amazing. Have you been here before?"

"Not for a while." Katie lowered her voice and glanced to the register and back. "That guy kind of scares me."

"I don't think he approved of your decision to skip the mustard."

Katie frowned at the idea that she might not have imagined a negative reaction after all.

"I'm not sure I approve either," Cameron said in a teasing tone. "You don't know what you're missing."

"I do. But I'm not missing it. And who doesn't like cheese on a burger?" She looked pointedly at his plate.

Cameron smiled. A bit of the tension lifted. Then he set down his food and eyed her seriously. "I don't know what to call you," he said.

Now they were getting to the real meat. "I like Katie and Katherine so it doesn't really matter to me. Whichever you like better."

"I was thinking about you as Katie on my way here, but when I look at you..."

Katie understood without him having to finish the sentence. He saw the woman he knew from work, the one he'd known as Katherine for two years.

"I guess I'm having trouble merging... um... you with you."

"Okay." There was some hope in his statement. It sounded as though he was willing to try. Katie wanted him to voice that more concretely before her hopes swelled too much. "Do you... Is that something you can get past?"

"Eventually," he said. "It's not like you're the only person I've known who has a nickname. The name won't be a problem."

The emphasis on the name not being a problem implied something else was. Katie braced herself. Cameron ate a French fry. Then another one. They were having dinner so he probably wasn't intentionally stalling. The pause wasn't as long as it felt.

"I've been going over everything in my head," he said. "There's something... I don't think it's my imagination that you started talking to me more at work right around the time you starting talking to me... not at work. That feels too coincidental."

Suspicious. He might as well have said it felt suspicious. And she had to agree with him thinking that. How could she explain that she'd entertained fantasies about him being the same guy without really believing it or admitting that was because she had a crush on him forever or that she'd been stringing along the other version of him to do it? Telling him she'd been about to agree to meet when she discovered who he was would sound hollow and far-fetched.

She squirmed trying to find words admitting her guilt without making it awful or unforgivable. "I did notice that you had the same first name. Obviously. I don't know how many Camerons are around, and it made me wonder. I didn't really think you could be the same guy, but I still hoped maybe I could get you to contradict something in one of your letters to be sure. I wanted to... I *didn't* want to be surprised by meeting someone I already sort of knew."

"You could have asked me," Cameron said. "Something as simple as where do you work would have told you."

Katie nodded, growing warmer under the dissection of her folly. "I didn't think I could do that without inviting the same questions."

"Oh. You wanted to find out who I was without letting me know who you were?" It was clear that he wasn't asking her to confirm the statement but to defend it.

There was no good defense. "It was cowardly, I know," Katie said. "But I thought I could prevent awkwardness at work if... um..."

Cameron jumped in while she tried to find words. "Because you planned to stop messaging me if you found out I was... me."

This me and me stuff was confusing. But it still sounded awful. Katie couldn't deny that was exactly what she planned to do when it was exactly what she had done. Cameron didn't seem to understand that she'd been trying to spare *him* the awkwardness.

"What changed your mind?" he asked. "I mean, you got away with it. I had no idea who you were. If you still aren't interested, you could have said no when I asked about dinner. Why did you confess?" He sounded justifiably confused. It seemed he hadn't joined her for dinner with hopes that their relationship might begin to blossom but simply because not knowing her motives was going to bother him.

Katie did have hopes, hopes that required her to be honest. She thought of the dreams and stories they'd shared in print and his acceptance of her old age and odd family. It all made her want to be honest. She could tell him without using embarrassing words like "crush" and "daydreams" and "extra cute when you're concentrating."

"You have it backwards," she said. "I was... I tried to get your attention a little back when you first started at EJ. You didn't seem interested in me at all. So when I... well, I thought *you'd* be disappointed, and it'd be easier if you just... didn't know. But then it seemed like maybe you changed your mind. I couldn't show up here with history only one of us knew. I had to confess."

He nodded slowly, the kind of nod that said he was thinking about what she said. He had a few bites while he processed it.

Katie's burger was tasty enough to provide some comfort while she waited. The tension had dissolved somewhat as well. Perhaps because her confession was more complete. She looked from her food to Cameron and back repeatedly, shyly trying to figure out what he was thinking.

His eyes met her gaze and held it. "You know about my bad experience dating someone from work. I had intentional blinders when I first started, determined not to... But you say you tried to get my attention?"

Cameron looked so happy and even flattered by that idea that it was easy for Katie to admit it with a nod.

"I kind of thought you might be lately and after... the other you dropped me, I thought it might be worth trying to find out if you were someone worth getting to know better. When you told me I was already getting to know you... it was, well, sort of good but also confusing."

"So you forgive me?" Katie asked hopefully.

"Yeah, I don't think there's anything to forgive now that..." Cameron set his burger back down without taking another bite. "It took me awhile to decide if I *believed* you. It felt like a trick. But it didn't make any sense that you'd back out when you did unless you really were surprised. I wondered how you couldn't know but then *I* didn't know. You even described yourself, and I didn't see it. That part I figured out though. You used very bland terms. You are not bland."

Not bland was hardly a compliment, except that Cameron said it in a way that emphasized he thought that was putting it mildly. It made Katie blush.

"Plus, you like Tichu," he said playfully. "Nothing else matters."

She laughed and finally relaxed. The mood lightened but not the conversation. They talked about some of the things they'd shared in print, policies at work, their families, even comfortably talked about the fears of meeting someone online in person. They discussed the rumor at work that Connie had inadvertently been double-billing a huge customer for months and the retraining was a show of accountability to go with some refunds. They talked about Tichu strategy. The food was gone and so were most of the other customers by the time Katie noticed the scary mustached guy glaring at them that it was nearly closing time. She left quite a bit happier than she'd arrived.

Cameron walked outside with her. They stood in front of Burger Brothers for a reluctant goodbye. Katie thought about stepping closer to invite a quick hug. A kiss on a public street wasn't right. She was too nervous to clarify all that without words, and maybe that wasn't possible anyway. Cameron told her he looked forward to *talking* more in the morning, and she knew what he meant. He sent the first message before she finished her getting ready for the day routine.

*I think I do like Katie better. But I will try to keep calling you Katherine at work. Not because it would be inappropriate but because I'm not sure I like the idea of anyone else trying to copy that familiarity. Our place smelled like bacon this morning. Elijah made a quiche. I told him it was about time he made something with bacon. I don't have much planned for today after church besides a few errands. What about you?*
*Cameron*

*I guess it's a good thing this new girl isn't a vegetarian. Has he actually cooked for her yet? I'm not too worried about us keeping things professional. Don't start making billing mistakes just to get me to come to your office more often.*
    *Katie*

*I know you're kidding, but that's a good idea. What if Connie actually stops bringing you in after your seminar?*

*It isn't my seminar, remember? I'm just doing the research and making the slides and the presentation notes. Why is lunch a good time for extra work?*

*I suppose it's better than overtime.*

*True. I'll try to look on the bright side. I guess it's a good thing we don't need Connie to give me an excuse to see you anymore.*

*On a more serious note, would you consider it unprofessional to start having lunch with me at work?*

*Or we could go to the January Café together, just not this week. I won't have time. Where do you normally eat?*

*At my desk. I would definitely move to either break room for you though.*

*How romantic. The west one is usually less crowded. I'll meet you there on Monday if we finish with time left to eat.*

*Okay. Are you confirming that plan so you can do something else now?*

*No. Just confirming for the sake of confirming. I'm available until you have to leave for church.*

*Hmm. What would you say about me meeting you at St. Jude's instead of going here?*

16

Audra opened the door and said, "Where have you been all week?"

The question wasn't surprising, but Katie hadn't expected it to be the first thing she said. "I've been roped into helping my boss with a project at work," Katie said. "He thinks half our lunch hours is the best time to work on it so I'd barely have time to drive to the January Café and back and not enough time to eat."

"Ah, so this was just a temporary absence?" Audra motioned Katie towards the card table as Alison had arrived ahead of her.

"Yeah. We finished this afternoon. And by we, I mean he presented what was mostly my work with a nod to me at the end for my *input.*"

"That's annoying," Violet said.

Katie shrugged off the sympathy. "People were generally annoyed at having to sit through it so it's actually better I don't get credit."

The women had gathered around the table as they greeted each other with Alison across from Katie. The two of them hadn't been partners yet as they were the least experienced players. Katie smiled at her questioningly, and Alison nodded that she was up for the challenge.

Violet was shuffling.

"Okay, I have an idea," Audra said.

The cards stilled in Violet's hands before she began to pass them out. She raised an eyebrow at Audra in that moment.

"Katie, since you haven't been making the drive to Tindee all week, you should come tomorrow. You haven't seen my paintings or Alison's store." Audra let this soft admonishment sink in before she continued. "If you come a little before noon, you can see everything and we'll go next door for lunch after."

It was a good idea. Katie was genuinely curious about both of those sights, and there was nothing wrong with lunch with friends. She still hesitated because of a hint of defensiveness in Audra's voice. That, and the fact that Violet seemed to be avoiding eye contact, suggested there was something more to the invitation.

"It's a good idea," Audra said in response to the delay.

Alison had her forehead wrinkled in thought, too. "It is," she said, "which makes it odd that you sound like you're making a hard sell."

Audra fanned out her cards in a deliberately casual manner. "Do you want to come or not?"

"Sure." Katie was now curious about the ulterior motive as well. She would need to wait until the next day to learn Audra's plan as she let it drop as soon as she got her answer, focusing on the game instead. Katie let her mind mostly stick to Tichu. Some good luck, and possibly strategy, gave her and Alison an early lead. The others caught up during some light conversation. Katie generally enjoyed the game and the company except that she began to feel that she had missed her chance.

Audra was collecting the cards to put them away. That meant someone was about to suggest it was time to interrupt the guys' game. Katie had planned to let the others know that her relationship with Cameron was shifting before they were all together. She wanted to bring it up casually though and not make some big announcement. She could have mentioned that she'd been having her short lunches with him. Saying something right as she walked through the door

146

felt like a big announcement. There hadn't been any other time during the game that felt like a natural transition.

And now they were all moving towards the door without anyone even saying they should. Not that there was any doubt about where they were going.

"Something on your mind, Katie?" Audra said. "I mean, Katherine."

Audra obviously corrected herself in preparation for calling her Katherine in front of Cameron. It was a perfect opportunity to explain that kind of discretion was no longer necessary. Except that saying she was dating Cameron as she was caught staring into space might make her seem like a moony, mushy-brained, lovesick… And Audra was three seconds from ringing her brothers' doorbell anyway.

Katie just smiled and shook her head.

****

Cameron almost jumped at the sound of the doorbell. He'd been expecting it, and it still startled him. He hadn't had a chance to mention his discovery about Katie and Katherine. He hadn't given many details about his online relationship, like her name, before it went sour. Suddenly saying she was Katherine wasn't something he could mention, he'd have to explain. He didn't want to explain. The ladies probably knew by now though. One of them would surely say something to him about it. Then they could do the explaining. He wasn't excited about that, but he was excited about seeing Katie. The conflicting sentiments made him off-balance.

Katie came in with Audra and smiled at him with her eyes. They seemed to communicate a secret. Even though he didn't know what it was, it was more interesting than anything else in the room. When she broke the eye contact, he was able to take in that she had changed to more casual clothes since work and pulled her hair into a ponytail. It still boggled his mind that this beautiful woman had been behind all the entertaining stories and profound thoughts he'd spent months relishing. Perhaps he hadn't needed to work so hard to keep his expectations low.

"Still a game going on here," Trevor said.

Cameron glanced across the table at his partner, who he expected to see chastising his sister for interrupting. But Trevor was looking at Cameron. Alison wasn't behind him. Had she left already? There was a card on the table, and it appeared to be Cameron's turn. Had Trevor led the six or had Ryan? Luckily, it didn't matter. Cameron had an eight to unload and neither of the others would expect to win with a six anyway.

Audra was checking the score. Looking over the previous rounds would keep her distracted until they finished this one. Then she'd probably say something that highlighted the recent romantic turn in the group. Would she ask if he'd been enjoying his work lunches more because she knew Katie was now sharing them? Or would she insinuate that his evenings had been much improved? He and Katie had resumed regular messaging, sometimes while on the phone. He was an unapologetic introvert, never one for unnecessary chitchat. But every word exchanged with Katie felt valuable.

"Are you going to deal or are you going to let him shuffle all night?"

Logan was the one shuffling, and Ryan had asked the question. He wasn't talking to Trevor. Cameron employed his powers of deduction and reached for the cards.

"I think I would have risked it," Violet said.

"It was pretty late for there to have been no aces," Katie said. "Someone was bound to have a pair."

They were talking about the game, not anyone's love life. That was a welcome surprise. And Katie had intelligent commentary. She stepped nearer to his elbow to watch his cards as he fanned them out. He tried to concentrate on not making any careless mistakes in front of her. He glanced up at Audra as she set down the phone and looked at Logan's hand instead. She bit the side of her lip against a wince at his passing choices. Previous conversations revealed that she liked to hold out for a long straight. She might be disappointed that he wasn't going that route. Cameron's seven-card straight felt a touch safer.

A few tricks into the round, Audra's hand came up and floated a moment before landing on Logan's shoulder. It seemed she had stopped herself from pointing at one of his cards. Before he could guess what that could mean for his own cards, Cameron was hit by the thought of Katie's hand resting on his shoulder the same way. Would that feel like support or simply heighten his awareness of the woman behind him, the woman he'd been spending even more time thinking about than he'd spent wondering about before they met. Or before he knew that they'd met.

"I wish I knew if those tens were gonna win."

The note of impatience in Trevor's voice was speaking to Cameron even if he wasn't. There were triple tens on the table, near the center, not close to whoever had played them. Trevor only had two cards left. He'd be annoyed if Cameron beat them when he was about to go out. But if they belonged to someone on the other team – like Logan who also only had two cards – Trevor would expect Cameron to beat them if he could. When did Logan get down to two cards? And how long could Cameron deliberate before they thought he wasn't paying attention? Wait a minute. He didn't have anything that topped the tens. "Pass," he said.

Logan claimed the tens and played a three. Cameron tried not to look at Audra again. Reading the other players was part of the game, but reading spectators was sort of a gray area. It was difficult to remember not to look at someone in front of you. And Logan did allow her to stand there when he knew she couldn't hide her thoughts. Trevor passed. He probably had a pair. Ryan played an ace. He still had most of his cards, and Violet wasn't giving any of them away. She was looking over Cameron's shoulder. At Katie. She seemed to be studying Katie.

Maybe Violet was going to be the one to put the two of them on the spot, the one who pointed out that Katie was standing a little closer to Cameron than she had the previous week. Cameron didn't think that was his imagination.

They'd talked about her watching his cards. Katie wanted to be sure he really didn't mind. She'd said she was completely freaked out the week she recognized him. If he hadn't seen that, he could certainly trust her not to reveal the presence of a dragon. She was reserved but not secretive. The shock of learning that he knew Katie in real life had initially felt like deception. But she was so open about her own shock that she'd built up more trust. Her admission that she'd been interested in him for some time bolstered his ego and…

A throat cleared. Sounded like Trevor. Oh, right. Cameron's turn came after Ryan. "Pass," he said.

Logan and Ryan went out first and second to significantly extend their lead. Audra recorded the score with a congratulatory smile at Logan. "Only a hundred and fifty from victory," she said.

"And how many dozen are in that?" Ryan asked.

Audra made a disgusted groan. "You said you weren't going to bring that up."

"I said I wouldn't tell anyone at work."

She narrowed her eyes at the technicality but seemed to be fighting a laugh.

"I went into the kitchen and found Audra pulling cookies out of a bag. When I asked her what she was doing, she said, 'I lost count. I need twenty-four and oh, my goodness, that's two dozen.' Then she crumpled like she'd just done something incredibly dumb."

"I did." Audra returned the phone to the table and sounded resigned to telling the whole tale. "Someone asked for twenty-four cookies. There are a dozen on each pan, and I started taking from a pan that had either five or seven on it. I was trying to remember that so I could do some math if I lost count, but then I couldn't remember if there were seven cookies and five blanks or the other way around.

Right as Ryan asked, it hit me that if I'd simply started with a full pan, I wouldn't've had to count anything. I blame the customer," she said. "Who asks for twenty-four when you want two dozen?"

"Someone who knows basic conversions," Trevor said.

"I know it," Audra snapped. "I was just rushing and... not thinking."

There were a few smiles. No one judged Audra too harshly as most people had experienced similar momentary lapses.

Cameron was mostly focused on the cards being dealt. The round was not looking promising. He glanced back to see if Katie agreed before he realized she couldn't commiserate without sharing with the entire room. *Speaking of momentary lapses*, he thought.

Not that he could kick himself too hard for wanting an excuse to look at her.

Ryan called a very confident-sounding Tichu.

"I think that's our cue to leave," Audra said. She waved Violet and Katie towards the door.

"Why?" Violet asked.

"If they get the Tichu, the game might end this round so..."

That explained nothing, and yet Violet nodded. "Good luck," she said to Ryan as she followed Audra.

Katie trailed after the others, smiling as though she was amused that something didn't make sense.

"Do you guys know what that was about?" Ryan asked.

"Huh?" Trevor looked up from his hand.

"Audra seemed to think they needed to leave before we finish," Ryan explained. "Why would that be an issue?"

Trevor rolled his eyes. "You're going to hurt yourself trying to guess what Audra is thinking."

The astute observation ended the speculation. The round went as poorly as Cameron predicted, and he and Trevor lost. It was late enough that they called it a night. Logan stopped him on their way to their cars.

"Hang on a minute," he said. "I'm afraid I do know why Audra dragged the girls out in a hurry."

Cameron waited to hear how this was something he needed to know.

"She wanted me to talk to you on the way out." Logan sighed to illustrate that his arm had been twisted. "I'm supposed to ask you if you want to have lunch with us tomorrow. She has some sort of matchmaking plan with you and Katherine. I'm not supposed to tell you that part of course. But you should have all the facts before you decide if you have other plans."

Maybe Katie hadn't told anyone matchmaking was unnecessary. And maybe Audra hatched this plan before she found out and hadn't told Logan. But she still got out of the way for him to do his part. Regardless of what Audra knew, Cameron thought this sounded like a chance to spend some time with Katie. They'd talked about getting together over the weekend but hadn't made specific plans. He could play along with this one. "I can do lunch," he said.

Logan accepted the answer and told him what time to meet them at Alison's shop.

17

Katie lived farther away. Cameron didn't know if her head start would get her home first so he started a longer message, figuring she'd be home by the time he was ready to send it.

*I've been invited to be a third wheel at lunch with Logan and Audra. That probably would have sounded suspicious even if he hadn't told me that Audra has matchmaking plans at the same time. Did she ask you to do something tomorrow?*

*I'm wondering what you told her. Does she still think I don't know who you are? I mean, it's okay if you didn't tell her. I haven't told anyone besides my mom, and you know I was vague there. I don't think I can hold her off much longer on coming over for dinner. She was thrilled to let me off the hook for a date, but she's getting insistent that I grab a meal there. There will be so much grilling, and I don't mean the food.*

*I thought everyone would know tonight because when I said I would tell the guys if it came up, you said it would come up as soon as Audra knew. That's what brings me back to asking about her. How was your night in general?*
*Cameron*

*No, I didn't tell anyone. There just wasn't a natural segue. I knew they were going to tease me, and I didn't want to bring that into your game. I know you didn't want the guys to give you a hard time. Audra asked me to come look at her*

*paintings tomorrow. Actually, it was more like she told me I
needed to see them and stop making Alison feel bad for not
being interested in her family's store at the same time. I like
the ones I've seen so I'm sure it'll be fun. I'm supposed to be
there at 11:45. What about you? I think we should let Audra
think she's being subtle until... I'm not sure when. I bet there
will be a good moment to reveal that we're already together.
The game was good in general. I had a hand with two bombs
and still didn't go out. I think it was just that bad, but maybe
I misplayed.*

*Katie*

*Yes, I've had that hand. It's awful. I don't think it would be
so bad to have the guys know I'm not hopeless. Logan just
said a little before noon. I can pick you up and we can just go
in one at a time if you don't want it to be obvious right away
that we came together.*

*Cameron*

*It doesn't make any sense for you to drive significantly out of
your way to get me when you live practically on my way there.
I'll be the one driving. No arguments, it's bedtime. I'll see
you tomorrow. I'm looking forward to it. And maybe the
paintings, too.*

\*\*\*\*

Cameron tried not to look out the window for her. At least
not very often. If he knew when she arrived though, she wouldn't
have to get out and walk up the sidewalk to let him know. It was
practical, but it felt sappy. When Katie's car pulled up, he closed and
locked his door quietly behind himself, then jogged towards the front
of the building. He still wasn't fast enough.

Katie had gotten out and was already on the sidewalk. She
stopped to wait for him. A few steps away, he was tempted to greet
her with a hug or maybe even a kiss. But he hadn't initiated any
physical contact yet and decided the time wasn't quite right to start.
He simply said, "Hi," and they got into her car.

154

It was a fairly small car. The proximity made Cameron regret that he hadn't attempted some minimal touch. Except that the minimum was probably a handshake, and that would have just been weird. The inside of her car smelled nicer than his. The fact that he noticed the faint scent was probably also weird. Perhaps he should try some conversation. There was a wooden rosary wrapped around her rear-view mirror. "Nice rosary," he said. "But I thought only old people did that."

Cameron cringed as the words left his mouth. He forgot that she was sensitive about being older than he was. Katie was not going to appreciate the joke.

Fortunately, she laughed and said, "An old person did do that. My dad hung it there. He said it's supposed to remind me to drive carefully. I wouldn't have put it up myself, but I... Well, this is my second car, and I did move it from the first one so I guess I got used to it."

"I have St. Peter."

"In your car?" Katie asked.

"It's a little plastic statue, maybe four inches tall." Cameron pictured it as he described it. "Brown robe and sandals, keys that are half his size. I've had it since I was little and don't even remember where I got it. When I was packing up to move out of my parents' house, I was trying to decide if that was something I wanted to take with me, and I looked at it probably more closely than I had in a long time. I realized it's actually supposed to be a key chain. There's a hole for a ring in the strap holding his keys where you can add yours. It's too big to be a key chain though so I stashed it in my glove box because that somehow seemed appropriate. It's been there ever since."

"And does it remind you to drive safely?" Her tone was teasing.

"I don't need the reminder," Cameron said, which he was happy to see made her smile. "But there was one time – I had just put it in there – and this guy nearly ran me off the road, and I was

155

muttering some not very nice things and… I remembered the statue and that St. Peter, who has the keys, could hear me. Not that the statue could hear me, obviously, but… you know."

"I do," Katie said. She was pulling into a parking lot. Three blocks from the shop with the paintings.

"Next Love is next door to the January Café," he said. "I bet there are closer spots." He wondered if she was that concerned about preventing Audra from seeing them arrive together.

"Maybe." Katie shut off her car and turned to him. "There are plenty of spaces in this lot though. I park here when I come for lunch. I like to save the places in front of the stores for people who might need them more than I do. I'm healthy and not in a hurry or buying anything heavy and…" She shrugged off the rest of the thought.

Cameron was impressed by the small sacrifice. He would try to remember the next time he lucked into a great parking spot that maybe it wasn't luck. Maybe someone deliberately passed it by. Or maybe he could do the same. Being impressed by the attractive woman two feet away made him want to reach for her. But again, it wasn't quite right. There was a plan. "So which of us is going in first?" he asked.

"Well… Audra told me 11:45 and Logan just expects you a few minutes before noon. I guess it makes sense for you to give me about a five-minute head start."

He nodded and opened the car door as he said, "I'll walk *really* slowly."

Katie smiled at him over the top of the car. "See you soon."

She had on a gray hoodie that she zipped as she began to walk away. Dried leaves bounced across the parking lot in the chilly breeze. Cameron hardly heard them as his pulse picked up in his ears. He wanted to catch up to Katie, grab her hand, and walk by her side. But he was going to stay back and support her wish to surprise Audra. He waited what might have been thirty seconds, then moved his feet one small step at a time after Katie. He got to the corner in time to see her enter the building. Then he paused again. He was in front of a pizza place, and yeast and spices were in the air. Cameron breathed in the aroma a few times before he resumed his slow walk.

A car parked next to him that he recognized as Logan's. That was an excuse to stop again.

Logan jumped out and jogged around the front of the car. "Hey, man, looks like you're dragging your feet."

"Uh…" Cameron was dragging his feet but not out of the reluctance Logan likely suspected.

"I don't have to mention I saw you if you want to back out of Audra's game."

"No, that's… I was enjoying the scent of this place."

Logan inhaled the plausibility and nodded. He motioned for Cameron to follow him down the street. The furniture store had a fairly ornate door that Logan opened and held for Cameron.

"Hello, gentlemen," Elaine Brachy said exuberantly as they were still in the doorway.

Cameron got the impression she'd seen them coming. He and Logan returned the greeting together.

"*You've* come to the right place." Her eyes fixed meaningfully on Cameron. He was afraid Alison's mom was about to slip into full-on sales mode. He didn't need a table or a chair or anything else she might try to show him. But she tilted her head towards the back of the shop where Alison and Audra were talking with Katie. There was something he needed back there.

Logan led him through the maze of wooden cabinets and desks and such. There was a faint sawdusty smell in the air. Cameron's eyes were fixed on Katie as he walked towards her. She didn't see him coming. She wasn't pretending not to notice for anyone's benefit. It was clear that she was engrossed in the artwork on the wall. She was so engrossed that it was almost as though she'd completely forgotten about him in the few minutes since she'd walked away. Cameron felt a flash of jealousy and a ridiculous need to assert his presence. He held his place at Logan's side anyway.

"Hello," Logan said. "Look who I just happened to bump into outside."

Audra frowned at his transparent tone. But then she smiled at Cameron. "Hi, Cameron. What do you think of my work on display?"

"It does actually look a little different lined up on the wall," he said. She occasionally brought a newly finished piece when she showed up to interrupt Tichu, but he'd never seen a collection of her work together. "More professional."

She smiled and said, "Katherine likes it, too."

Katie was staring at a picture, but she nodded at the mention of her name. "There's a face in this bunch of wildflowers," she said softly. "I didn't see it until Alison pointed it out and now… There's no way flowers would naturally grow so that… and yet it looks so natural."

"Since we're all here around lunchtime, maybe the four of us could have lunch together as soon as we're done?" Audra sent an apologetic glance at Alison, who didn't appear remotely offended. She was working and likely knew there was a setup in progress. She might have even been relieved to be excluded.

"That's why I'm here," Logan said.

Audra looked hopefully between Cameron and Katie.

Cameron nodded that he was okay with food.

Katie swept her eyes distractedly over the people around her before moving on to the next painting. "Yeah, whatever," she said. "I want to look at a few more first."

Alison quietly stepped away to resume a sanding project nearby. Logan winced slightly in sympathy that Katie didn't seem enthusiastic or even aware that she was being fixed up. Audra shifted her weight, looking torn between the compliment of Katie being so interested in her art and disappointed that she wasn't more interested in her brilliant, spur-of-the-moment idea for a double date.

"We could just go next door," Audra said. "All four of us like the January Café, right?" She seemed determined to get Katie's take on the obvious pairings within the foursome. When Katie didn't even nod, she turned to Cameron. "Okay with you?"

A very strong impulse told him it was the moment to let everyone know he was more than okay with Katie. He stepped forward and slipped one hand onto the side of her face to gently turn her head towards him. He had her attention well enough that she read the intent because she wasn't startled when he kissed her. She was clearly ready to kiss him back. She was smiling when he pulled back and obviously unconcerned with the paintings or anything else in the world.

Until she noticed Audra's eyes popping out of her head. Then Katie started laughing and said, "He knows who I am, Audra. I told him last week and we've been talking quite a bit since."

Audra put her eyes back in place and rolled them. "Why didn't you tell me? I put a lot of effort into trying to help you guys out, and you didn't even need my help." She tried to sound exasperated but couldn't hide the amusement in her voice.

"Uh... who are you?" Logan's expression said he wasn't even sure that was the right question.

"We don't just know each other from work," Katie said.

"Oh," Logan said, though he clearly didn't understand.

"Don't worry," Audra said, "we'll explain everything over lunch." She gave Katie a look that told everyone where she expected the details to come from.

"Okay," Katie said, as she let Cameron entwine their fingers. Her attention was divided, but he could tell he had the biggest share and was feeling pretty proud of himself.

Audra gestured for everyone to start moving towards the exit. "The good news is this means all three of you can help me with my next project."

"Your next... oh, wait." Logan groaned. "You don't mean another matchmaking project, do you?"

A broad grin was her only response.

"Tell me as little as possible," Logan said, "so I can honestly say I knew as little as possible when it blows up."

Audra lightly punched his arm. "It's not going to blow up." She cast her eyes back over Katie and Cameron's joined hands. "I know a good couple when I see one."

"A good couple doesn't need your help," Logan said.

Cameron agreed, but he wasn't about to jump into the discussion. He had heard the hint that Logan wasn't the only one who might be pulled into something. But at the moment, he didn't care. He only cared that his own match was already at his side.

~~ The End ~~


~~ Visit amandahammbooks.com to find out about more books. ~~